AT THE OUTERMOST REACHES

The decades-long war between Earth and Mars is over, leaving the red planet desolate and uninhabited. Some of the stations in the incredible Martian subway system are sealed and others are guarded by armies of robots. Behind those doors lies the last, and most closely guarded secret on Mars...

The lone survivor of an expedition to Venus returns to Earth to find an utterly empty world. All living creatures have disappeared—except for one beautiful young woman with strangely vacant eyes...

The distant future has arrived. While man has been evolving, his canine friends have undergone their own remarkable transformation into a race of super-dogs. Fully as intelligent as twentieth-century humans, they have become the doers of the world. And one of them holds the fate of North America in his paws...

BEFORE THE UNIVERSE

BEFORE THE UNIVERSE

and other stories

Frederik Pohl
and
C. M. Kornbluth

The best of the early work of science fiction's most famous team of collaborators, including four stories never before in book form.

BEFORE THE UNIVERSE

A Bantam Book / July 1980

Book designed by Cathy Marinaccio

The stories contained in this volume were all previously published:

"Mars Tube," copyright 1941 by Fictioneers, Inc.;
"Trouble In Time," copyright 1940 by Fictioneers, Inc.;
"Vacant World," copyright 1940 by Fictioneers, Inc.;
"Best Friend," copyright 1941 by Fictioneers, Inc.;
"Nova Midplane," copyright 1940 by Fictioneers, Inc.,
"The Extrapolated Dimwit," copyright 1942
by Columbia Publications, Inc.

ISBN 0-553-11042-X

Published simultaneously in the United States and Canada

Bantam Books are published by Bantam Books, Inc. Its trademark,
consisting of the words "Bantam Books" and the portrayal of a bantam,
is Registered in U.S. Patent and Trademark Office and in other countries.
Marca Registrada. Bantam Books, Inc., 666 Fifth Avenue, New York,
New York 10019.

PRINTED IN THE UNITED STATES OF AMERICA

0 9 8 7 6 5 4 3 2 1

CONTENTS

INTRODUCTION

In the late 1930s in New York City, a bunch of us kids, fans anxious to become pros, joined together in The Futurian Society of New York. Don Wollheim was the "old man" of the group. He had been old enough to vote in the presidential election of 1936; most of the rest of us wouldn't make it for several years thereafter. The other members included Dirk Wylie, Robert W. Lowndes, Isaac Asimov, Richard Wilson, John B. Michel—well, the story of the Futurians has been told often enough.* And to us was drawn, around 1938, a young, plump, bright fellow from the farthest north part of Manhattan you can be in without striking the Bronx, Cyril Kornbluth.

In 1939 I became editor of two P*R*O*F*E*S*S*I*O*N*A*L science fiction magazines called *Astonishing Stories* and *Super Science Stories*. They were low-budget projects in every respect. The magazines sold for a dime and fifteen cents respectively, and paid their writers (and me) accordingly. In order to acquire enough stories to put an issue together without leaving a sizeable fraction of the pages blank, I had to beat the bushes for cheap talent. The first and most obvious place to beat was within The Futurian Society. In putting together one

---

* And is the subject of a forthcoming nonfiction book by Damon Knight.

issue, I found myself ten thousand words short, and had something like $35 left in my budget to buy a story with. So I took my troubles to the fannish commune on Bedford Avenue, Brooklyn, where half a dozen of the Futurians lived, and Cyril Kornbluth and Dick Wilson undertook to fill the hole for me. They stayed up all night, each banging away on his own typewriter. I have never known the exact circumstances, but as I understand it Dick Wilson started on page one and Cyril started on page twenty, and somehow they managed to make the ends match up in the middle. It came out to a precise ten thousand words, and was entitled "Stepsons of Mars." They signed it with the joint pen name of "Ivar Towers"—the name of the commune, you see, was "The Ivory Tower"—and I published it. I would not say the story was good. But even at that stage both Cyril and Dick were gifted enough with words so that it wasn't utterly bad. The reader mail dealt with it no more harshly, or kindly, than with any of the other stories in the issue.

I don't think it was the first Futurian collaboration. We had all been collaborating with each other from time to time. Any two Futurians might match up to produce a story. If they found the going rough, they might well call in any other, or any several others. There was one story in which, if my memory does not play me false, something like seven of us claimed a share before it was published. As an editor I was hospitable to all Futurians, being one of them myself. So were Don Wollheim and Doc Lowndes, when shortly thereafter they acquired magazines of their own to edit; but we managed to sell stories from time to time even to non-Futurian editors. I made sales, alone or in collaboration, to *Amazing*, *Astounding*, and *Planet Stories*. Wollheim and Michel sold to *Astounding*, Lowndes to *Unknown*, Asimov was beginning to sell to everybody, mostly alone (he was always a strange one, Isaac was), but once or twice in collaboration with me. Etcetera. There was a lot of talent in the Futurians. And a lot of it was concentrated in the person of Cyril Kornbluth.

I remember some of Cyril's nonprofessional production at that time. Strange little essays, quirky "almost-stories,"poetry. Some of it was doggerel, but funny doggerel, as in the one he called "Gym Class":

> One, two, three, four,
> Flap your arms and prance,
> In stinky shirt and stinky shoes
> And stinky little pants.

Some of it was lushly sexual, as in a poem—I think it was called "Elephanta," but I cannot now say why—which began:

> How long, my love, shall I behold this wall
> Between our gardens, yours the rose
> And mine the swooning lily....

And some of it was simply brilliant. As far as I know, it is almost all lost, but it would repay someone to search through the Futurian fan magazines of the period to see if any might still be found.

The first published story by Cyril and me was *Before the Universe*. (It is included in this volume.) We worked out an assembly line procedure: I wrote an "action chart"—essentially a plot outline, with some indication of characters and setting—from which Cyril wrote a first draft, which I then revised and retyped ... and, more often than not, published. When "Before the Universe" reached print, the reader mail was satisfactory, if not wildly enthusiastic, and we decided to continue the series with "Nova Midplane" and "The Extrapolated Dimwit," also both included here.

At the same time we were writing other stories together, sometimes with a third party; and we were both also writing extensively with others or alone. I really don't know how many stories we wrote during the period covered by this book, which all in all was only about three years, late 1939 through 1942. According to my records, about twenty-six science fiction stories which I wrote (in whole or in part) did get published during that period. (Cyril and most of the other Futurians stayed pretty close to science fiction. I wandered. I was also writing for the detective, horror, fantasy, air war, sports, and love pulps at that time—everything but Westerns, which I simply could not bring myself to do. It wasn't so much that I wanted to appear in them as that I wanted to test myself to see if I could survive outside the SF ambience.) Cyril's total must have been similar.

Nearly everything Cyril and I wrote together got published. After all, once I was finished revising it there was at least one editor who, by definition, was pleased with it. So if it didn't sell somewhere else the first time or two out, it always sold to me. But there were a few stories which we did not finish for one reason or another (some of which we came back to much later, and are in the other volume*), and at least one story which we finished but never published, because it got lost. It was called "Under the Sequoias. "(Neither Cyril nor I had ever seen a sequoia, but then we hadn't actually seen the surface of Mars, either.) It had something to do with a superior race of beings who lived underground. Actually I think it was one of the best stories we wrote together at that time, but that may be only memory beautifying truth. At any rate, I have little hope of ever reading it again.

We wrote another story about a man who used some chemical to precipitate oxygen out of the air in the form of snow, and jell the ocean as warm ice (ah, there, Kurt Vonnegut), but unfortunately it had to do with the impending crisis between the United States and Japan, and before we got it printed Pearl Harbor put it out of date. So we tore it up.

All the other early stories we wrote in collaboration without other partners (plus two on which we called in a third hand) are herein. I hope you will read them gently, gentle reader. They are our youth.

---

* *Critical Mass*, Bantam Books.

BEFORE THE UNIVERSE

MARS-TUBE

Nearly all the stories in this volume were written for, and appeared in, one of the two magazines I was editing at the time, **Astonishing Stories** *and* **Super Science Stories***. There are good reasons why an editor should not write for himself, but there are good reasons why he should, too. One is for balance. When, as writer, I write for myself, as editor, what I usually write is the kind of story I wish I had to print but don't seem to get enough of from other sources. "Mars-Tube" is one of those. I like colorful extraterrestrial adventure. I also like humorous SF. I* **never***, as an editor, have enough stories which combine these two qualities, and so over the years I've written a good many such stories to print myself. "Mars-Tube" was one of the first.*

I. After Armageddon

Ray Stanton set his jaw as he stared at the molded lead seal on the museum door. Slowly, he deciphered its inscription, his tongue stumbling over the unfamiliar sibilants of the Martian language as he read it aloud before translating. "To the—strangers from the third planet—who have won their—bitter—triumph—we of Mars charge you—not to wantonly destroy—that which you will find—within this

1

door ... Our codified learning—may serve you—better than we ourselves—might have done."

Stanton was ashamed of being an Earthman as he read this soft indictment. "Pathetic," he whispered. "Those poor damned people."

His companion, a slight, dark-haired girl who seemed out of place in the first exploratory expedition to visit Mars after the decades-long war that had annihilated its population, nodded in agreement. "The war was a crying shame," she confirmed. "But mourning the dead won't bring them back. To work, Stanton!"

Stanton shook his head dolefully, but copied the seal's inscription into his voluminous black archaeologist's notebook. Then he tore off the seal and tentatively pushed the door. It swung open easily, and an automatic switch snapped on the hidden lights as the two people entered.

Both Stanton and Annamarie Hudgins, the girl librarian of the expedition, had seen many marvels in their wanderings over and under the red planet, for every secret place was open to their eyes. But as the lights slowly blossomed over the colossal hall of the library, he staggered back in amazement that so much stately glory could be built into one room.

The synthetic slabs of gem-like rose crystal that the Martians had reserved for their most awesome sanctuaries were flashing from every wall and article of furnishing, winking with soft ruby lights. One of the typically Martian ramps led up in a gentle curve from their left. The practical Annamarie at once commenced to mount it, heading for the reading-rooms that would be found above. Stanton followed more slowly, pausing to examine the symbolic ornamentation in the walls.

"We must have guessed right, Annamarie," he observed, catching up with her. "This one's the central museum-library for sure. Take a look at the wall-motif."

Annamarie glanced at a panel just ahead, a bas-relief done in the rose crystal. "Because of the ultima symbol, you mean?"

"Yes, and because—well, look." The room in which they found themselves was less noble than the other, but considerably more practical. It was of radical design, corridors converging like the spokes of a wheel on a focal point where they stood. Inset in the floor—they were almost standing on it—was the ultima symbol, the quadruple linked circles which indicated preeminence. Stanton peered down a corridor lined with racks of wire spools. He picked up a spool and stared at its title-tag.

"Where do you suppose we ought to start?" he asked.

"Anywhere at all," Annamarie replied. "We've got lots of time, and no way of knowing what to look for. What's the one in your hands?"

"It seems to say 'The Under-Eaters'—whatever that may mean," Stanton juggled the tiny "book" undecidedly. "That phrase seems familiar somehow. What is it?"

"Couldn't say. Put it in the scanner and we'll find out." Stanton obeyed, pulling a tiny reading-machine from its cubicle. The delicacy with which Stanton threaded the fragile wire into its proper receptacle was something to watch. The party had ruined a hundred spools of records before they'd learned how to adjust the scanners, and Stanton had learned caution.

Stanton and his companion leaned back against the book-racks and watched the fluorescent screen of the scanner. A touch of the lever started its operation. There was a soundless flare of light on the screen as the wire made contact with the scanning apparatus, then the screen filled with the curious wavering peak-and-valley writing of the Martian graphic language.

By the end of the third "chapter" the title of the book was still almost as cryptic as ever. A sort of preface had indicated that "Under-Eaters" was a name applied to a race of underground demons who feasted on the flesh of living Martians. Whether these really existed or not Stanton had no way of telling. The Martians had made no literary distinction between fact and fiction, as far as could be learned. It had been their opinion that anything except pure thought-transference was only approximately true, and that it would be useless to distinguish between an intentional and an unintentional falsehood.

But the title had no bearing on the context of the book, which was a kind of pseudo-history with heavily allusive passages. It was a treatment of the Earth-Mars war: seemingly it had been published only a few months before the abrupt end to hostilities. One rather tragic passage, so Stanton thought, read:

"A special meeting of the tactical council was called on (an untranslatable date) to discuss the so-called new disease on which the attention of the enemy forces has been concentrating. This was argued against by (a high official) who demonstrated conclusively that the Martian intellect was immune to nervous diseases of any foreign order, due to its high development through telepathy as cultivated for (an untranslatable number of) generations. A minority report submitted that this very development itself would render the Martian intellect more liable to succumb to unusual strain. (A medical authority) suggested that certain forms of insanity were contagious by means of telepathy, and that the enemy-spread disease might be of that type."

Stanton cursed softly: "Damn Moriarity and his rocket ship. Damn Sweeney for getting killed and damn and double-damn the World Congress for declaring war on Mars!" He felt like a murderer, though he knew he was no more than a slightly pacifistic young exploring archaeologist. Annamarie nodded sympathetically but pointed at the screen. Stanton looked again and his imprecations were forgotten as he brought his mind to the problem of translating another of the strangely referential passages:

"At this time the Under-Eaters launched a

bombing campaign on several of the underground cities. A number of subterranean caves were linked with the surface through explosion craters and many of the sinister creations fumbled their way to the surface. A corps of technologists prepared to reseal the tunnels of the Revived, which was done with complete success, save only in (an untranslatable place-name) where several Under-Eaters managed to wreak great havoc before being slain or driven back to their tunnels. The ravages of the Twice-Born, however, were trivial compared to the deaths resulting from the mind diseases fostered by the flying ships of the Under-Eaters, which were at this time ..."

The archaeologist frowned. There it was again. Part of the time. "Under-Eaters" obviously referred to the Earthmen, the rest of the time it equally obviously did not. The text would limp along in style-less, concise prose and then in would break an obscure reference to the "Creations" or "Twice-Born" or "Raging Glows."

"Fairy tales for the kiddies," said Annamarie Hudgins, snappinq off the scanner.

Stanton replied indirectly: "Put it in the knapsack. I want to take it back and show it to some of the others. Maybe they can tell me what it means." He swept a handful of other reading-bobbins at random into the knapsack, snapped it shut, and straightened. "Lead on, Mac-Hudgins," he said.

Of the many wonders of the red planet, the one that the exploration party had come to appreciate most was the colossal system of subways which connected each of the underground cities of Mars.

With absolute precision the web of tunnels and gliding cars still functioned, and would continue to do so until the central controls were found by some Earthman and the vast propulsive mechanisms turned off.

The Mars-Tube was electrostatic in principle. The perfectly round tunnels through which the subway sped were studded with hoops of charged metal.

The analysis of the metal hoops and the generators for the propulsive force had been beyond Earthly science, at least as represented by the understaffed exploring party.

Through these hoops sped the single-car trains of the Mars-Tube, every four minutes through every hour of the long Martian day. The electrostatic emanations from the hoops held the cars nicely balanced against the pull of gravity; save only when they stopped for the stations, the cars never touched anything more substantial than a puff of air. The average speed of the subway, stops not included, was upwards of five hundred miles an hour. There were no windows in the cars, for there would have been nothing to see through them but the endless tunnel wall slipping smoothly and silently by.

So easy was the completely automatic operation that the men from Earth could scarcely tell when the car was in motion, except by the signal panel that dominated one end of the car with its blinking lights and numerals.

Stanton led Annamarie to a station with ease and assurance. There was only one meaning to the tear-drop-shaped guide signs of a unique orange color that were all over Mars. Follow the point of a sign like that anywhere on Mars and you'd find yourself at a Mars-Tube station—or what passed for one.

Since there was only one door to a car, and that opened automatically whenever the car stopped at a station, there were no platforms. Just a smaller or larger anteroom with a door also opening automatically, meeting the door of the tube-car.

A train eventually slid in, and Stanton ushered Annamarie through the sliding doors. They swung themselves gently onto one of the excessively broad seats and immediately opened their notebooks. Each seat had been built for a single Martian, but accommodated two Terrestrials with room to spare.

At perhaps the third station, Annamarie, pondering the implications of a passage in the notebook, looked up for an abstracted second—and froze.

"Ray," she whispered in a strangled tone. "When did that come in?"

Stanton darted a glance at the forward section of the car, which they had ignored when entering. Something—something animate—was sitting there, quite stolidly ignoring the Terrestrials. "A Martian," he whispered to himself, his throat dry.

It had the enormous chest and hips, the waspish waist and the coarse, bristly hairs of the Martians. But the Martians were all dead—

"It's only a robot," he cried more loudly than was necessary, swallowing as he spoke. "Haven't you seen enough of them to know what they look like by now?"

"What's it doing here?" gulped Annamarie, not over the fright.

As though it were about to answer her question itself, the thing's metallic head turned, and its blinking eyes swept incuriously over the humans. For a long second it stared, then the dull glow within its eye-sockets faded, and the head turned again to the front. The two had not set off any system of reflexes in the creature.

"I never saw one of them in the subway before," said Annamarie, passing a damp hand over her sweating brow.

Stanton was glaring at the signal panel that dominated the front of the car. "I know why, too," he said. "I'm not as good a linguist as I thought I was—not even as good as I ought to be. We're on the wrong train—I read the code-symbol wrong."

Annamarie giggled. "Then what shall we do— see where this takes us or go back?"

"Get out and go back, of course," grumbled Stanton, rising and dragging her to her feet.

The car was slowing again for another station. They could get out, emerge to the surface, cross over, and take the return train to the library.

Only the robot wouldn't let them.

For as the car was slowing, the robot rose to its feet and stalked over to the door. "What's up?" Stanton whispered in a thin, nervous voice. Annamarie prudently got behind him.

"We're getting out here anyhow," she said. "Maybe it won't follow us."

But they didn't get out. For when the car had stopped, and the door relays clicked, the robot shouldered the humans aside and stepped to the door.

But instead of exiting himself, the robot grasped the edge of the door in his steel tentacles, clutched it with all his metal muscles straining, and held it shut!

"Damned if I can understand it," said Stanton. "It was the most uncanny thing—it held the door completely and totally shut there, but it let us get out as peaceful as playmates at the next stop. We crossed over to come back, and while we were waiting for a return car I had time to dope out the station number. It was seventh from the end of the line, and the branch was new to me. So we took the return car back to the museum. The same thing happened on the trip back—robot in the car; door held shut."

"Go on," said Ogden Josey, Roëntgenologist of the expedition. "What happened then?"

"Oh. We just went back to the library, took a different car, and here we are."

"Interesting," said Josey. "Only I don't believe it a bit."

"No?" Annamarie interrupted, her eyes narrowing. "Want to take a look?"

"Sure."

"How about tomorrow morning?"

"Fine," said Josey. "You can't scare me. Now how about dinner?"

He marched into the mess hall of the expedition base, a huge rotunda-like affair that might have been designed for anything by the Martians, but was given its present capacity by the explorers because it contained tables and chairs enough for a regiment. Stanton and Annamarie lagged behind.

"What do you plan to do tomorrow?" Stanton

inquired. "I don't see the point of taking Josey with us when we go to look the situation over again."

"He'll come in handy," Annamarie promised. "He's a good shot."

"A good shot?" squawked Stanton. "What do you expect we'll have to shoot at?"

But Annamarie was already inside the building.

II. Descent into Danger

"Hey, Sand-Man!" hissed Annamarie.

"Be right there," sleepily said Stanton. "This is the strangest date I ever had." He appeared a moment later dressed in the roughest kind of exploring garb.

The girl raised her brows. "Expect to go mountain-climbing?" she asked.

"I had a hunch," he said amiably.

"So?" she commented. "I get them too. One of them is that Josey is still asleep. Go rout him out."

Stanton grinned and disappeared into Josey's cubicle, emerging with him a few moments later. "He was sleeping in his clothes," Stanton explained. "Filthy habit."

"Never mind that. Are we all heeled?" Annamarie proudly displayed her own pearl-handled pipsqueak of a mild paralyzer. Josey produced a heat-pistol, while Stanton patted the holster of his five-pound blaster.

"Okay then. We're off."

The Martian subway service was excellent every hour of the day. Despite the earliness, the trip to the central museum station took no more time than usual—a matter of minutes.

Stanton stared around for a second to get his bearings, then pointed. "The station we want is over there—just beyond the large pink monolith. Let's go."

The first train in was the one they wanted. They

stepped into it, Josey leaping over the threshold like a startled fawn. Nervously he explained, "I never know when one of those things is going to snap shut on my—my cape." He yelped shrilly: "What's *that?*"

"Ah, I see the robots rise early," said Annamarie, seating herself as the train moved off. "Don't look so disturbed, Josey—we told you one would be here, even if you didn't believe us."

"We have just time for a spot of breakfast before things should happen," announced Stanton, drawing canisters from a pouch on his belt. "Here—one for each of us." They were filled with a syrup that the members of the Earth expedition carried on trips such as this—concentrated amino acids, fibrinogen, minerals, and vitamins, all in a sugar solution.

Annamarie Hudgins shuddered as she downed the sticky stuff, then lit a cigarette. As the lighter flared the robot turned his head to precisely the angle required to center and focus its eyes on the flame, then eye-fronted again.

"Attracted by light and motion," Stanton advised scientifically. "Stop trembling, Josey. There's worse to come. Say, is this the station?"

"It is," said Annamarie. "Now watch. These robots function smoothly and fast—don't miss anything."

The metal monster, with a minimum of waste motion, was doing just that. It had clumped over to the door; its monstrous appendages were fighting the relays that were to drive the door open, and the robot was winning. The robots were built to win—powerful, even by Earthly standards.

Stanton rubbed his hands briskly and tackled the robot, shoving hard. The girl laughed sharply. He turned, his face showing injury. "Suppose you help," he suggested with some anger. "I can't move this by myself."

"All right—heave!" gasped the girl, complying.

"Ho!" added Josey unexpectedly, adding his weight.

"No use," said Stanton. "No use at all. We

couldn't move this thing in seven million years." He wiped his brow. The train started, then picked up speed. All three were thrown back as the robot carelessly nudged them out of its way as it returned to its seat.

"I think," said Josey abruptly, "we'd better go back by the return car and see about the other side of the station."

"No use," said the girl. "There's a robot on the return, too."

"Then let's walk back," urged Josey. By which time the car had stopped at the next station. "Come on," said Josey, stepping through the door with a suspicious glance at the robot.

"No harm in trying," mused Stanton as he followed with the girl. "Can't be more than twenty miles."

"And that's easier than twenty Earth miles," cried Annamarie. "Let's go."

"I don't know what good it will do though," remarked Stanton, ever the pessimist. "These Martians were thorough. There's probably a robot at every entrance to the station, blocking the way. *If* they haven't sealed up the entrances entirely."

There was no robot at the station, they discovered several hours and about eight miles later. But the entrance to the station that was so thoroughly and mysteriously guarded was—no more. Each entrance was sealed; only the glowing teardrop pointers remained to show where the entrance had been.

"Well, what do we do now?" groaned Josey, rubbing an aching thigh.

Stanton did not answer directly. "Will you look at that," he marvelled, indicating the surrounding terrain. The paved ground beneath them was seamed with cracks. The infinitely tough construction concrete of the Martians was billowed and rippled, stuck through with jagged ends of metal reinforcing I-beams. The whole scene gave the appearance of total devastation—as though a natural catastrophe had

come along and wrecked the city first; then the sur-
vivors of the disaster, petulantly, had turned their
most potent forces on what was left in sheer dis-
heartenment.

"Must have been bombs," suggested the girl.

"Must have been," agreed the archaeologist.
"Bombs and guns and force beams and Earth—Mars-
quakes, too."

"You didn't answer his question, Ray," reminded Annamarie. "He said: 'What do we do
now?'"

"I was just thinking about it," he said, eyeing
one of the monolithic buildings speculatively. "Is
your Martian as good as mine? See if you can make
out what that says."

"That" was a code-symbol over the sole door
to the huge edifice. "I give up," said Annamarie with
irritation. "What does it say?"

"Powerhouse, I think."

"Powerhouse? Powerhouse for what? All the
energy for lighting and heating the city comes from
the sun, through the mirrors up on the surface. The
only thing they need power for down here—the only
thing— Say!"

"That's right," grinned Stanton. "It must be for
the Mars-Tube. Do you suppose we could find a way
of getting from that building into the station?"

"There's only one way to find out," Annamarie
parroted, looking for Josey for confirmation. But Josey was no longer around. He was at the door to the
building, shoving it open. The others hastened after
him.

III. Pursuit

"Don't wiggle, Annamarie," whispered Josey plain-
tively. "You'll fall on me."

"Shut up," she answered tersely. "Shut up and get out of my way." She swung herself down the Martian-sized manhole with space to spare. Dropping three feet or so from her hand-hold on the lip of the pit, she alighted easily. "Did I make much noise?" she asked.

"Oh, I think Krakatoa has been louder when it went off," Stanton replied bitterly. "But those things seem to be deaf."

The three stood perfectly still for a second, listening tensely for sounds of pursuit. They had stumbled into a nest of robots in the powerhouse, apparently left there by the thoughtful Martian race to prevent entrance to the mysteriously guarded subway station via this route. What was in that station that required so much privacy? Stanton wondered. Something so deadly dangerous that the advanced science of the Martians could not cope with it, but was forced to resort to quarantining the spot where it showed itself? Stanton didn't know the answers, but he was very quiet as a hidden upsurge of memory strove to assert itself. Something that had been in the bobbin-books . . . "The Under-Eaters." That was it. Had they anything to do with this robot *cordon sanitaire*?

The robots had not noticed them, for which all three were duly grateful. Ogden nudged the nearest to him—it happened to be Annamarie—and thrust out a bony finger. "Is *that* what the Mars-Tube looks like from inside?" he hissed piercingly.

As their eyes became acclimated to the gloom—they dared use no lights—the others made out the lines of a series of hoops stretching out into blackness on either side ahead of them. No lights anywhere along the chain of rings; no sound coming from it.

"Maybe it's a deserted switch line, one that was abandoned. That's the way the Tube ought to look, all right, only with cars going along it," Stanton muttered.

"Hush!" it was Annamarie. "Would that be a car coming—from the left, way down?"

Nothing was visible, but there was the faintest of sighing sounds. As though an elevator car, cut loose from its cable, were dropping down its shaft far off there in the distance. "It sounds like a car," Stanton conceded. "What do you think, Og— Hey! Where's Josey?"

"He brushed me, going toward the Tube. Yes— there he is! See him? Bending over between those hoops!"

"We've got to get him out of there! Josey!" Stanton cried, forgetting about the robots in the light of this new danger. "Josey! Get out of the Tube! There's a train coming!"

The dimly visible figure of the Roëntgenologist straightened and turned toward the others querulously. Then as the significance of that rapidly mounting *hiss-s-s-s* became clear to him, he leaped out of the tube, with a vast alacrity. A split second later the hiss had deepened to a high drone, and the bulk of a car shot past them, traveling eerily without visible support, clinging to and being pushed by the intangible fields of force that emanated from the metal hoops of the Tube.

Stanton reached Josey's form in a single bound. "What were you trying to do, imbecile?" he grated. "Make an early widow of your prospective fiancee?"

Josey shook off Stanton's grasp with dignity. "I was merely trying to establish that that string of hoops was the Mars-Tube, by seeing if the power-leads were connected with the rings. It—uh, it was the Tube; that much is proven," he ended somewhat lamely.

"Brilliant man!" Stanton started to snarl, but Annamarie's voice halted him. It was a very small voice.

"You loudmouths have been very successful in attracting the attention of those animated pile-drivers," she whispered with the very faintest of breaths. "If you will keep your lips zipped for the next little while maybe the robot that's staring at us over the rim of the pit will think we're turbogenerators or something and go away. Maybe!"

Josey swiveled his head up and gasped. "It's there—it's coming down!" he cried. "Let's leave here!"

The three backed away toward the tube, slowly, watching the efforts of the machine-thing to descend the precipitous wall. It was having difficulties, and the three were beginning to feel a bit better, when—

Annamarie, turning her head to watch where she was going, saw and heard the cavalcade that was bearing down on them at the same time and screamed shrilly. "Good Lord—the cavalry!" she yelled. "Get out your guns!"

A string of a dozen huge, spider-shaped robots of a totally new design were charging down at them, running swiftly along the sides of the rings of the Tube, through the tunnel. They carried no weapons, but the three soon saw why—from the ugly snouts of the egg-shaped bodies of the creatures protruded a black cone. A blinding flash came from the cone of the first of the new arrivals; the aim was bad, for overhead a section of the cement roof flared ghastly white and commenced to drop.

Annamarie had her useless paralyzer out and firing before she realized its uselessness against metal beings with no nervous systems to paralyze. She hurled it at the nearest of the new robots in a highly futile gesture of rage.

But the two men had their more potent weapons out and firing, and were taking a toll of the spider-like monstrosities. Three or four of them were down, partially blocking the path of the oncoming others; another was missing all its metal legs along one side of its body, and two of the remainder showed evidence of the accuracy of the Earthmen's fire.

But the odds were still extreme, and the built-in blasters of the robots were coming uncomfortably close.

Stanton saw that, and shifted his tactics. Holstering his heavy blaster, he grabbed Annamarie and shoved her into the Mars-Tube, crying to Josey to follow. Josey came slowly after them, turning to fire again and again at the robots, but with little effect. A quick look at the charge-dial on the butt of his heat-gun showed why; the power was almost exhausted.

He shouted as much to Stanton. "I figured that would be happening—now we run!" Stanton cried back, and the three sped along the Mars-Tube, leaping the hoops as they came to them.

"What a time for a hurdle race!" gasped Annamarie, bounding over the rings, which were raised about a foot from the ground. "You'd think we would have known better than to investigate things that're supposed to be private."

"Save your breath for running," panted Josey. "Are they following us in here?"

Stanton swivelled his head to look, and a startled cry escaped him. "They're following us—but look!"

The other two slowed, then stopped running altogether and stared in wonder. One of the robots had charged into the Mars-Tube—and had been levitated! He was swinging gently in the air, the long metal legs squirming fiercely, but not touching anything.

"How— ?"

"They're metal!" Annamarie cried. "Don't you see—they're metal, and the hoops are charged. They must have some of the same metal as the Tube cars are made of in their construction—the force of the hoops acts on them, too!"

That seemed to be the explanation. . . . "Then we're safe!" gasped Josey, staggering about, looking for a place to sit.

"Not by a long shot! Get moving again!" And Stanton set the example.

"You mean because they can still shoot at us?" Josey cried, following Stanton's dog-trot nonetheless. "But they can't aim the guns—they seem to be built in, only capable of shooting directly forward."

"Very true," gritted Stanton. "But have you forgotten that this subway is in use? According to my calculations, there should be another car along in about thirty seconds or less—and please notice, there isn't any bypath anymore. It stopped back a couple of hundred feet. If we get caught here by a car, we get smashed. So—unless you want to go back and sign an armistice with the robots . . . ? I thought not—so we better keep going. Fast!"

The three were lucky—very lucky. For just when it seemed certain that they would have to run on and on until the bullet-fast car overtook them, or go back and face the potent weapons of the guard robots, a narrow crevice appeared in the side of the tunnel wall. The three bolted into it and slumped to the ground.

CRASH!

"What was that?" cried Annamarie.

"That," said Josey slowly, "was what happens to a robot when the fast express comes by. Just thank God it wasn't us."

Stanton poked his head gingerly into the Mars-Tube and stared down. "Say," he muttered wonderingly, "when we wreck something we do it good. We've ripped out a whole section of the hoops—by proxy, of course. When the car hit the robot they were both smashed to atoms, and the pieces knocked out half a dozen of the suspension rings. I would say, offhand, that this line has run its last train."

"Where do you suppose this crevice leads?" asked Annamarie, forgetting the damage that couldn't be undone.

"I don't know. The station ought to be around here somewhere—we were running toward it. Maybe this will lead us into the station if we follow it. If it doesn't, maybe we can drill a tunnel from here to the station with my blaster."

Drilling wasn't necessary. A few feet in, the

scarcely passable crevice widened into a broad fissure, through which a faint light came from a wall-chart showing the positions and destinations of the trains. The chart was displaying the symbol of a Zeta train—the train that would never arrive.

"Very practical people, we are," Annamarie remarked with irony. "We didn't think to bring lights."

"We never needed them anywhere else on the planet—we can't be blamed too much. Anyway, the code-panel gives us a little light."

By the steady, dim red glow cast by the code-panel, the three could see the anteroom fairly clearly. It was disappointing. For all they could tell, there was no difference between this and any other station on the whole planet. But why all the secrecy? The dead Martians surely had a reason for leaving the guard-robots so thick and furious. But what was it?

Stanton pressed an ear to the wall of the anteroom. "Listen!" he snapped. "Do you hear— ?"

"Yes," said the girl at length. "Scuffling noises—a sort of gurgling too, like running water passing through pipes."

"Look there!" wailed Josey.

"Where?" asked the archaeologist naturally. The dark was impenetrable. Or was it? There was a faint glimmer of light, not a reflection from the code-panel, that shone through a continuation of the fissure. It came, not from a single source of light, but from several, eight or ten at least. The lights were bobbing up and down. "I'd swear they were walking!" marvelled Ray.

"Ray," shrieked the girl faintly. As the lights grew nearer, she could see what they were—pulsing domes of a purplish glow that ebbed and flowed in tides of dull light. The light seemed to shine from behind a sort of membrane, and the outer surfaces of the membrane were marked off with faces—terrible, savage faces, with carnivorous teeth projecting from mouths that were like ragged slashes edged in writhing red.

"Ray!" Annamarie cried again. "Those lights—they're the luminous heads of living creatures!"

"God help us—you're right!" Stanton whispered. The patterns of what he had read in the bobbin-books began to form a whole in his mind. It all blended in—"Under-Eaters," "Fiends from Below," "Raging Glows." Those weirdly cryptic creatures that were now approaching. And— "Good Lord!" Stanton ejaculated, feeling squeamishly sick. "Look at them—they look like human beings!"

It was true. The resemblance was not great, but the oncoming creatures did have such typically Terrestrial features as hairless bodies, protruding noses, small ears, and so forth, and did not have the unmistakable hourglass silhouette of the true Martians.

"Maybe that's why the Martians feared and distrusted the first Earthmen they saw. They thought we were related to these—things!" Stanton said thoughtfully.

"Mooning over it won't help us now," snapped Annamarie. "What do we do to get away from them? They make me nervous?"

"We don't do anything to get away. What could we do? There's no place to go. We'll have to fight—get out your guns!"

"Guns!" sneered Josey. "What guns? Mine's practically empty, and Annamarie threw hers away!"

Stanton didn't answer, but looked as though a cannonshell had struck him amidships. Grimly he drew out his blaster. "Then this one will have to do all of us," was all he said. "If only these accursed blasters weren't so unmanageable—there's at least an even chance that a bad shot will bring the roof down on us. Oh, well—I forgot to mention," he added casually, "that, according to the records, the reason that the true Martians didn't like these things was that they had the habit of *eating* their victims. Bearing that in mind, I trust you will not mind my chancing a sudden and unanimous burial for us all." He drew the blaster and carefully aimed it at the first of the oncoming group. He was already squeezing the trigger when Josey grabbed his arm. "Hold on, Ray!" Josey whispered. "Look what's coming."

The light-headed ones had stopped their inexorable trek toward the Terrestrials. They were bunched fearfully a few yards within the fissure, staring beyond the three humans, into the Mars-Tube.

Three of the spider-robots, the Tube-tenders, were there. Evidently the destruction of one of their number, and the consequent demolition of several of the hoops, had short-circuited this section of the track so that they could enter it and walk along without fear.

There was a deadly silence that lasted for a matter of seconds. The three from Earth cowered as silently as possible where they were, desirous of attracing absolutely no attention from either side. Then—Armageddon!

The three robots charged in, abruptly, lancing straight for the luminous-topped bipeds in the crevasse. Their metal legs stamped death at the relatively impotent organic creatures, trampling their bodies until they died. But the cave-dwellers had their methods of fighting, too; each of them carried some sort of instrument, hard and heavy-ended, with which they wreaked havoc on the more delicate parts of the robots.

More and more "Raging Glows" appeared from the crevasse, and it seemed that the three robots, heavily outnumbered, would go down to a hard-fought but inevitable "death"—if that word could be applied to a thing whose only life was electromagnetic. Already there were better than a score of the strange bipeds in the cavern, and destruction of the metal creatures seemed imminent.

"Why don't the idiotic things use their guns?" Annamarie shuddered.

"Same reason I didn't—the whole roof might come down. Don't worry—they're doing all right. Here come some more of them."

True enough. From the Mars-Tube emerged a running bunch of the robots—ten or more of them.

The slaughter was horrible—a carnage made even more unpleasant by the fact that the dimness of the cavern concealed most of the details. The fight was in comparative silence, broken only by the faint metallic clattering of the workings of the robots, and an occasional thin squeal from a crushed biped. The cave-dwellers seemed to have no vocal organs.

The robots were doing well enough even without guns. Their method was simply to trample and bash the internal organs of their opponents until the opponent had died. Then they would kick the pulped corpse out of the way and proceed to the next.

The "Hot-Heads" had had enough. They broke and ran back down the tunnel from which they had come. The metal feet of the robots clattered on the rubble of the tunnel floor as they pursued them at maximum speed. It took only seconds for the whole of the ghastly running fight to have traveled so far from the humans as to be out of sight and hearing. The only remnants to show it had ever existed were the mangled corpses of the cave-dwellers, and one or two wrecked robots.

Stanton peered after the battle to make sure it was gone. Then, mopping his brow, he slumped to a sitting position and emitted a vast "Whew!" of relief. "I have seldom been so sure I was about to become dead," he said pensively. "Divide and rule is what I always say—let your enemies fight it out among themselves. Well, what do we do now? My curiosity is sated—let's go back."

"That," said the girl sternly, "is the thing we are most not going to do. If we've come this far we can go a little farther. Let's go on down this tunnel and see what's there. It seems to branch off down farther; we can take the other route from that of the robots."

Josey sighed. "Oh, well," he murmured resignedly. "Always game, that's me. Let's travel."

"It's darker than I ever thought darkness could be, Ray," Annamarie said tautly. "And I just thought of something. How do we know *which* is the other route—the one the robots didn't take?"

"A typical question," snarled Stanton. "So you get a typical answer: I don't know. Or, to phrase it differently, we just have to put ourselves in the robots' place. If you were a robot, where would you go?"

"Home," Ogden answered immediately. "Home and to bed. But these robots took the tunnel we're in. So let's turn back and take the other one."

"How do you know?"

"Observation and deduction. I observed that I am standing in something warm and squishy, and I deduced that it is the corpse of a recent lighthead."

"No point in taking the other tunnel, though," Annamarie's voice floated back. She had advanced a few steps and was hugging the tunnel wall. "There's an entrance to another tunnel here, and it slopes back the way we came. I'd say, offhand, that the other tunnel is just an alternate route."

"Noise," said Stanton. "Listen."

There was a scrabbling, chittering, quite indescribable sound, and then another one. Suddenly, terrific squalling noises broke the underground silence and the three ducked as they sensed something swooping down on them and gliding over their heads along the tunnel.

"What was that?" yelped Josey.

"A cat-fight, I think," said Stanton. "I could hear two distinct sets of vocables, and there were sounds of battle. Those things could fly, glide, or jump—probably jump. I think they were a specialized form of tunnel life adapted to living, breeding, and fighting in a universe that was long, dark, and narrow. Highly specialized."

Annamarie giggled hysterically. "Like the bread-and-butterfly that lived on weak tea with cream in it."

"Something like," Stanton agreed.

Hand in hand, they groped their way on through the utter blackness. Suddenly there was a grunt from Josey, on the extreme right. "Hold it," he cried, withdrawing his hand to finger his damaged nose. "The tunnel seems to end here."

"Not end," said Annamarie. "Just turns to the left. And take a look at what's there!"

The men swerved and stared. For a second no one spoke; the sudden new vista was too compelling for speech.

"Ray!" finally gasped the girl. "It's incredible! It's *incredible!*"

There wasn't a sound from the two men at her sides. They had rounded the final bend in the long tunnel and come out into the flood of light they had seen. The momentary brilliance staggered them and swung glowing spots before their eyes.

Then, as the effects of persistence of vision faded, they saw what the vista actually was. It was a great cavern, the hugest they'd ever seen on either planet—and by tremendous odds the most magnificent.

The walls were not of rock, it seemed, but of slabs of liquid fire—liquid fire which, their stunned eyes soon saw, was a natural inlay of incredible winking gems.

Opulence was the rule of this drusy cave. Not even so base a metal as silver could be seen here; gold was the basest available. Platinum, iridium, little pools of shimmering mercury dotted the jewel-studded floor of the place. Stalactites and stalagmites were purest rock-crystal.

Flames seemed to glow from behind the walls colored by the emerald, ruby, diamond, and topaz. "How can such a formation occur in nature?" Annamarie whispered. No one answered.

"'There are more things in heaven and under it—'" raptly misquoted Josey. Then, with a start, "What act's that from?"

It seemed to bring the others to. "Dunno," chorused the archaeologist and the girl. Then, the glaze slowly vanishing from their eyes, they looked at each other.

"Well," breathed the girl.

In an abstracted voice, as though the vision of the jewels had never been seen, the girl asked, "How do you suppose the place is lighted?"

"Radioactivity," said Josey tersely. There seemed to be a tacit agreement—if one did not mention the gems neither would the others. "Radioactive minerals and maybe plants. All this is natural formation. Weird, of course, but here it is."

There was a feeble, piping sound in the cavern.

"Can this place harbor life?" asked Stanton in academic tones.

"Of course," said Josey, "any place can." The thin, shrill piping was a little louder, strangely distorted by echoes.

"Listen," said the girl urgently. "Do you hear what I hear?"

"Of course not," cried Stanton worriedly. "It's just my—I mean our imagination. I can't be hearing what I think I'm hearing."

Josey had pricked his hears up. "Calm down, both of you," he whispered. "If you two are crazy—so am I. That noise is something—somebody—singing Gilbert and Sullivan. 'A Wand'ring Minstrel, I', I believe the tune is."

"Yes," said Annamarie hysterically. "I always liked that number." Then she reeled back into Stanton's arms, sobbing hysterically.

"Slap her," said Josey, and Stanton did, her head rolling loosely under the blows. She looked up at him.

"I'm sorry," she said, the tears still on her cheeks.

"I'm sorry, too," echoed a voice, thin, reedy, and old; "and I suppose you're sorry. Put down your

guns. Drop them. Put up your hands. Raise them. I
really am sorry. After all, I don't *want* to kill you."

IV. Marshall Ellenbogan

They turned and dropped their guns almost immediately, Stanton shrugging off the heavy power-pack
harness of his blaster as Josey cast down his useless
heat-pistol. The creature before them was what one
would expect as a natural complement to this cavern.
He was weird, pixyish, dressed in fantastic points
and tatters, stooped, wrinkled, whiskered, and palely
luminous. *Induced radioactivity*, Stanton thought.

"Hee," he giggled. "Things!"

"We're men," said Josey soberly. "Men like—
like you." He shuddered.

"Lord," marvelled the pixy to himself, his gun
not swerving an inch. "What won't they think of
next! Now, now, you efts—you're addressing no pul-
ing creature of the deep. I'm a man and proud of it.
Don't palter with me. You shall die and be reborn
again—eventually, no doubt. I'm no agnostic, efts.
Here in this cavern I have seen—oh the things I have
seen." His face was rapturous with holy bliss.

"Who are you?" asked Annamarie.

The pixy started at her, then turned to Josey
with a questioning look. "Is your friend all right?"
the pixy whispered confidentially. "Seems rather
effeminate to me."

"Never mind," the girl said hastily. "What's
your name?"

"Marshall Ellenbogan," said the pixy surpris-
ingly. "Second Lieutenant in the United States Navy.
But," he snickered, "I suspect my commission's ex-
pired."

"If you're Ellenbogan," said Stanton, "then you
must be a survivor from the first Mars expedition.
The one that started the war."

"Exactly," said the creature. He straightened
himself with a sort of somber dignity. "You can't

know," he groaned, "you never could know what we went through. Landed in a desert. Then we trekked for civilization—all of us, except three kids that we left in the ship. I've often wondered what happened to them." He laughed. "Civilization! Cold-blooded killers who tracked us down like vermin. Killed Kelly, Keogh. Moley. Jumped on us and killed us—like that." He made a futile attempt to snap his fingers. "But not me—not Ellenbogan—I ducked behind a rock and they fired on the rock and rock and me both fell into a cavern. I've wandered—Lord! how I've wandered. How long ago was it, efts?"

The lucid interval heartened the explorers. "Fifty years, Ellenbogan," said Josey. "What did you live on all that time?"

"Moss-fruits from the big white trees. Meat now and then, eft, when I could shoot one of your light-headed brothers." He leered. "But I won't eat. I haven't tasted meat for so long now ... Fifty years. That makes me seventy years old. You efts never live for more than three or four years, you don't know how long seventy years can be."

"We aren't efts," snapped Stanton. "We're human beings same as you. I swear we are! And we want to take you back to Earth where you can get rid of that poison you've been soaking into your system! Nobody can live in a radium-impregnated cave for fifty years and still be healthy. Ellenbogan, for God's sake be reasonable!"

The gun did not fall or waver. The ancient creature regarded them shrewdly, his head cocked to one side. "Tell me what happened," he said at length.

"There was a war," said the girl. "It was about you and the rest of the expedition—armed this time, because the kids you left in the ship managed to raise Earth for a short time when they were attacked, and they told the whole story. The second expedition landed, and—well, it's not very clear. We only have the ship's log to go by, but it seems to have been about the same with them. Then the Earth governments raised a whole fleet of rocketships, with everything in the way of guns and ray-projectors they could hold installed. And the Martians broke down the atomic-power process from one of the Earth ships they'd captured, and *they* built a fleet. And there was a war, the first interplanetary war in history. For neither side ever took prisoners. There's some evidence that the Martians realized they'd made a mistake at the beginning after the war had been going only about three years, but by that time it was too late to stop. And it went on for fifty years, with rocketships getting bigger and faster and better, and new weapons being developed ... Until finally we developed a mind-disease that wiped out the entire Martian race in half a year. They were telepathic, you know, and that helped spread the disease."

"Good for them," snarled the elder. "Good for the treacherous, devilish, double-dealing rats ... And what are you people doing here now?"

"We're an exploring party, sent by the new all-Earth confederation to examine the ruins and salvage what we can of their knowledge. We came on you here quite by accident. We haven't got any evil intentions. We just want to take you back to your own world. You'll be a hero there. Thousands will cheer you—millions. Ellenbogan, put down your gun. Look—we put ours down!"

"Hah!" snarled the pixy, retreating a pace. "You had me going for a minute. But not any more!" With a loud click, the pixy thumbed the safety catch of his decades-old blaster. He reached back to the power pack he wore across his back, which supplied energy for the weapon, and spun the wheel to maximum output. The power-jack was studded with rubies which, evidently, he had hacked with diamonds into something resembling finished, faceted stones.

"Wait a minute, Ellenbogan," Stanton said desperately. "You're the king of these parts, aren't you? Don't you want to keep us for subjects?"

"Monarch of all I survey, eft. Alone and undisputed." His brow wrinkled. "Yes, eft," he sighed, "you are right. You efts are growing cleverer and cleverer—you begin almost to understand how I feel. Sometimes a king is lonely—sometimes I long for companionship—on a properly deferential plane, of course. Even you efts I would accept as my friends if I did not know that you wanted no more than my blood. I can never be the friend of an eft. Prepare to die."

Josey snapped: "Are you going to kill the girl, too?"

"Girl?" cried the pixy in amazement. "What girl?"

His eyes drifted to Annamarie Hùdgins. "Bless me," he cried, his eyes bulging. "Why, so he is! I mean, she is! That would explain it, of course, wouldn't it?"

"Of course," said Stanton. "But you're not going to kill her, are you?"

"If she were an eft," mused the pixy, "I certainly would. But I'm beginning to doubt that she is. In fact, you're probably all almost as human as I am. However—" He mistily surveyed her.

"Girl," he asked dreamily, "do you want to be a queen?"

"Yes, sir," said Annamarie, preventing a shudder. "Nothing would give me more pleasure."

"So be it," said the ancient, with great decision. "So be it. The ceremony of coronation can wait till later, but you are now ex officio my consort."

"That is splendid," cried Annamarie, "simply splendid." She essayed a chuckle of pleasure, but which turned out to be a dismal choking sound. "You've—you've made me positively the happiest woman under Mars."

She walked stiffly over to the walking monument commemorating what had once been a man, and kissed him gingerly on the forehead. The pixy's seamed face glowed for more reasons that the induced radioactivity as Stanton stared in horror.

"The first lesson of a queen is obedience," said the pixy fondly, "so please sit there and do not address a word to these unfortunate former friends of yours. They are about to die."

"Oh," pouted Annamarie. "You are cruel, Ellenbogan."

He turned anxiously, though keeping the hair-trigger weapon full on the two men. "What troubles you, sweet?" he demanded. "You have but to ask and it shall be granted. We are lenient to our consort."

The royal "we" already thought Stanton. He wondered if the ancient would be in the market for a coat of arms. Three years of freehand drawing in his high school in Cleveland had struck Stanton as a dead waste up till now; suddenly it seemed that it might save his life.

"How," Annamarie was complaining, "can I be a *real* queen without any subjects?"

The pixy was immediately suspicious, but the girl looked at him so blandly that his ruffles settled down. He scratched his head with the hand that did not hold the blaster. "True," he admitted. "I hadn't thought of that. Very well, you may have a subject. One subject."

"I think two would be much nicer," Annamarie said a bit worriedly, though she retained the smile.

"One!"

"Please—two?"

"One! One is enough. Which of these two shall I kill?"

Now was the time to start the sales-talk about the coat-of-arms, thought Stanton. But he was halted in mid-thought, the words unformed, by Annamarie's astonishing actions. Puckering her brow so very daintily, she stepped over to the pixy and slipped an arm about his waist. "It's hard to decide," she remarked languidly, staring from one to the other, still with her arm about the pixy. "But I think—

"Yes. I think—kill *that* one." And she pointed at Stanton.

Stanton didn't stop to think about what a blaster could do to a promising career as artist by appointment to Mars' only monarch. He jumped—lancing straight as a string in the weak Martian gravity, directly at the figure of the ancient. He struck and bowled him over. Josey, acting a second later, landed on top of him, the two piled onto the pixy's slight figure. Annamarie, wearing a twisted smile, stepped aside and watched quite calmly.

Oddly enough, the pixy had not fired the blaster.

After a second, Stanton's voice came smotheredly from the wriggling trio. He was addressing Josey. "Get up, you oaf," he said. "I think the old guy is dead."

Josey clambered to his feet, then knelt again to examine Ellenbogan. "Heart failure, I guess," he said briefly. "He was pretty old."

Stanton was gently prodding a swelling eye. "Your fault, idiot," he glared at Josey. "I doubt that one of your roundhouse swings touched Ellenbogan. And as for you, friend," he sneered, turning to Annamarie, "you have my most heartfelt sympathies. Not for worlds would I have made you a widow so soon. I apologize," and he bowed low, recovering himself with some difficulty.

"Did it ever occur to you," Annamarie said tautly—Stanton was astounded as he noticed she was trembling with a nervous reaction—"did it ever occur to you that maybe you owe me something? Because if I hadn't disconnected his blaster from the power-pack, you would be— "

Stanton gaped as she turned aside to hide a flood of sudden tears, which prevented her from completing the sentence. He dropped to one knee and ungently turned over the old man's body. Right enough—the lead between power-pack and gun was dangling loose, jerked from its socket. He rose again and, staring at her shaking figure, stepped unsteadily toward her.

Josey, watching them with scientific impersonality, upcurled a lip in the beginnings of a sneer. Then suddenly the sneer died in birth, and was replaced by a broad smile. "I've seen it coming for some time," more loudly than was necessary, "and I want to be the first to congratulate you. I hope you'll be very happy," he said ...

A few hours later, they stared back at the heap of earth under which was the body of the late Second Lieutenant Ellenbogan, U.S.N., and quietly made their way toward the walls of the cavern. Choosing a different tunnel mouth for the attempt, they began the long trek to the surface. Though at first Stanton and Annamarie walked hand-in-hand, it was soon arm-in-arm, then with arms around each other's waists, while Josey trailed sardonically behind.

TROUBLE IN TIME

"Trouble in Time" was the second story Cyril and I published in collaboration. (The first was "Before the Universe.") In most of these early stories I thought them up and "action-charted" them; Cyril wrote a complete first draft from my plot outline; and I revised them for publication. So the responsibility for structure and final form is mostly mine. What Cyril contributed was only the hardest part.

To begin at the beginning, everybody knows that scientists are crazy. I may be either mistaken or prejudiced, but this seems especially true of mathematico-physicists. In a small town like Colchester gossip spreads fast and furiously, and one evening the word was passed around that an outstanding example of the species Doctissimus Dementiae had finally lodged himself in the old frame house beyond the dog pound on Court Street, mysterious crates and things having been unloaded there for weeks previous.

Abigail O'Liffey, a typical specimen of the low type that a fine girl like me is forced to consort with in a small town, said she had seen the Scientist. "He had broad shoulders," she said dreamily, "and red hair, and a scraggly little mustache that wiggled up and down when he chewed gum."

"What would you expect it to do?"

She looked at me dumbly. "He was wearing a kind of garden coat," she said. "It was like a painter's, only it was all burned in places instead of having paint on it. I'll bet he discovers things like Paul Pasteur."

"Louis Pasteur," I said. "Do you know his name, by any chance?"

"Whose—the Scientist's? Clarissa said one of the expressmen told her husband it was Cramer or something."

"Never heard of him," I said. "Good night." And I slammed the screen door. Cramer, I thought—it was the echo of a name I knew, and a big name at that. I was angry with Clarissa for not getting the name more accurately, and with Abigail for bothering me about it, and most of all with the Scientist for stirring me out of my drowsy existence with remembrances of livelier and brighter things not long past.

So I slung on a coat and sneaked out the back door to get a look at the mystery man, or at least his house. I slunk past the dog pound, and the house sprang into sight like a Christmas tree—every socket in the place must have been in use, to judge from the flood of light that poured from all windows. There was a dark figure on the unkempt lawn; when I was about ten yards from it and on the verge of turning back, it shouted at me: "Hey, you! Can you give me a hand?"

I approached warily; the figure was wrestling with a crate four feet high and square. "Sure," I said.

The figure straightened. "Oh, so he's a she," it said. "Sorry, lady. I'll get a hand truck from inside."

"Don't bother," I assured it. "I'm glad to help." And I took one of the canvas slings as it took the other, and we carried the crate in, swaying perilously. "Set it here, please," he said, dropping his side of the crate. It *was* a he, I saw in the numerous electric bulbs' light, and from all appearances the Scientist, Cramer, or whatever his name was.

I looked about the big front parlor, bare of furniture but jammed with boxes and piles of machinery. "That was the last piece," he said amiably, noting my gaze. "Thank you. Can I offer you a scientist's drink?"

"Not—ethyl?" I cried rapturously.

"The same," he assured me, vigorously attacking a crate that tinkled internally. "How do you know?"

"Past experience. My alma mater was the Housatonic University, School of Chemical Engineering."

He had torn away the front of the crate, laying bare a neat array of bottles. "What's a C.E. doing in this stale little place?" he asked, selecting flasks and measures.

"Sometimes she wonders," I said bitterly. "Mix me an Ethyl Martini, will you?"

"Sure, if you like them. I don't go much for the fancy swigs myself. Correct me if I'm wrong." He took the bottle labeled C_2H_5OH. "Three cubic centimeters?"

"No—you don't start with the ethyl!" I cried. "Put four minims of fusel oil in a beaker." He complied. "Right—now a tenth of a grain of saccharine saturated in theine barbiturate ten percent solution." His hands flew through the pharmaceutical ritual. "And now pour in the ethyl slowly, and stir, don't shake."

He held the beaker to the light. "Want some color in that?" he asked, immersing it momentarily in liquid air from a double thermos.

"No," I said. "What are you having?"

"A simple fusel highball," he said, expertly pouring and chilling a beakerful, and brightening it with a drop of a purple dye that transformed the colorless drink into a sparkling beverage. We touched beakers and drank deep.

"That," I said gratefully when I had finished

coughing, "is the first real drink I've had since graduating three years ago. The stuff has a nostalgic appeal for me."

He looked blank. "It occurs to me," he said, "that I ought to introduce myself. I am Stephen Trainer, late of Mellon, late of Northwestern, late of Cambridge, sometime fellow of the Sidney School of Technology. Now you tell me who you are and we'll be almost even."

I collected my senses and announced, "Miss Mable Evans, late in practically every respect."

"I am pleased to make your acquaintance, Miss Evans," he said. "Won't you sit down?"

"Thank you," I murmured. I was about to settle on one of the big wooden boxes when he cried out at me.

"For God's sake—not there!"

"And why not?" I asked, moving to another. "Is that your reserve stock of organic bases?"

"No," he said. "That's part of my time machine."

I looked at him. "Just a nut, huh?" I said pityingly. "Just another sometimes capable fellow gone wrong. He thinks he knows what he's doing, and he even had me fooled for a time, but the *idée fixe* come out at last, and we see the man for what he is—mad as a hatter. Nothing but a time-traveler at the bottom of that mass of flesh and bone." I felt sorry for him, in a way.

His face grew as purple as the drink in his hand. As though he too had formed the association, he drained it and set it down. "Listen," he said. "I only know one style of reasoning that parallels yours in its scope and utter disregard of logic. Were you ever so unfortunate as to be associated with that miserable charlatan, Dr. George B. Hopper?"

"My physics professor at Housatonic," I said, "and whaddya make of that?"

"I am glad of the chance of talking to you," he said in a voice suddenly hoarse. "It's no exaggeration to say that for the greater part of my life I've wanted to come across a pupil of Professor Hopper. I've sat under him and over him on various faculties; we even went to Cambridge together—it disgusted both of us. And now at last I have the chance, and now you are going to learn the *truth* about physics."

"Go on with your lecture," I muttered skeptically.

He looked at me glassily. "I *am* going on with my lecture," he said. "Listen closely. Take a circle. What is a circle?"

"You tell me," I said.

"A circle is a closed arc. A circle is composed of an infinite number of straight lines, each with a length of zero, each at an angle infinitesmally small to its adjacent straight lines."

"I should be the last to dispute the point," I said judiciously. He reached for the decanter and missed. He reached again grimly, his fist opening and closing, and finally snapping shut on its neck. "Will you join me once more?" he asked graciously.

"Granted," I said absently, wondering what was going around in my head.

"*Now*—one point which we must get quite clear in the beginning is that all circles are composed of an in— "

"You said that already," I interrupted.

"Did I?" he asked with a delighted smile. "I'm brighter than I thought." He waggled his head fuzzily. "Then do you further admit that, by a crude Euclidean axiom which I forget at the moment, all circles are equal?"

"Could be—but so help me, if— " I broke off abruptly as I realized that I was lying full length on the floor. I shuddered at the very thought of what my aunt would say to *that*.

"The point I was about to make," he continued without a quaver, "was that if all circles are *equal*, all circles can be traversed at the same expenditure of effort, money, or what have you." He stopped and gaped at me, collecting his thoughts. "All circles can be traversed, also, with the same amount of *time*! No matter whether the circle be the equator or the head of a pin! Now do you see?"

"With the clarity appalling. And the time-travelling . . . ?"

"Ah—er—yes. The time-travelling. Let me think for a moment." He indicated thought by a Homeric configuration of his eyebrows, forehead, cheeks, and chin. "Do you know," he finally said with a weak laugh, "I'm afraid I've forgotten the connection. But my premise is right, isn't it? If it takes the same time to traverse any two circles, and one of them is the universe, and the other is my time wheel— " His voice died under my baleful stare.

"I question your premise vaguely," I said. "There's nothing I can exactly put my finger on, but I *believe* it's not quite dry behind the ears."

"Look," he said. "You can question it as much as you like, but it *works*. I'll show you the gimmicks."

We clambered to our feet. "There," he pointed to the box I had nearly sat upon, "there lies the key to the ages." And he took up a crowbar and jimmied the top off the crate.

I lifted out carefully the most miscellaneous collection of junk ever seen outside a museum of modern art. "What, for example," I asked, gingerly dangling a canvas affair at arms' length, "does this thing do?"

"One wears it as a belt," he said. I put the thing on and found that it resolved itself into a normal Sam Browne belt with all sorts of oddments of things dangling from it.

"Now," he said, "I have but to plug this into a wall socket, and then, providing you get on the time-wheel, out you go like a light— *pouf!*"

"Don't be silly," I said. "I'm practically out now in the first place, in the second place I don't care whether I go out *pouf* or *splash*—though the latter

is more customary—and in the third place I don't
believe your silly old machine works anyway. I
dare you to make me go *pouf*—I just dare
you!"

"All right," he said mildly. "Over there is the
time-wheel. Get on it."

The time-wheel reminded me of a small hand-
turned merry-go-round. I got on it with a good will,
and he made it turn. Then he plugged in the lead to
a wall socket, and I went out like a light—*pouf!*

There are few things more sobering than time-travel.
On going *pouf* I closed my eyes, as was natural. Possibly I screamed a little, too. All I know is when I
opened my eyes they were bleary and aching, and
certainly nowhere very near the old house past the
dog-pound on Court Street. The locale appeared to
be something like Rockefeller Center, only without
fountains.

I was standing on polished stones—beautifully
polished stones which seemed to set the keynote of
the surroundings. Everything was beautiful and
everything was polished. Before me was a tall, tall
building. It was a dark night, and there seemed to be
a great lack of illumination in this world of tomorrow.

I followed my nose into the building. The revolving door revolved without much complaint, and
did me the favor of turning on the lights of the lobby.

There were no people there; there were no people anywhere in sight. I tried to shout, and the
ghastly echo from the still darkened sections made
me tremble to my boots. I didn't try again, but very
mousily looked about for an elevator or something.
The something turned out to be a button in a vast
column, labeled in plain English, "Slavies'
ring."

I rang, assuring myself that doing so was no
confession of inferiority, but merely the seizing of
an offered opportunity. All the lobby lights went out,
then, but the column was glowing like mother-of-

pearl before a candle. A sort of door opened, and I walked through. "Why not?" I asked myself grimly.

I seemed to be standing on a revolving staircase—but one that actually revolved! It carried me up like a gigantic corkscrew at a speed that was difficult to determine. It stopped after a few minutes, and another door opened. I stepped through and said "Thank you" nicely to the goblins of the staircase, and shuddered again as the door slammed murderously fast and hard.

Lights go again at my landing place—I was getting a bit more familiar with this ridiculous civilization. Was everybody away at Bermuda for the summer? I wondered. Then I chattered my teeth.

Corpses! Hundreds of them! I had had the bad taste, I decided, to land in the necropolis of the world of tomorrow.

On slabs of stone they lay in double rows, great lines of them stretching into the distance of the huge chamber into which I had blundered. Morbid curiosity moved me closer to the nearest stiff. I had taken a course in embalming to get my C.E., and I pondered on the advances of that art.

Something hideously like a bed lamp clicked on as I bent over the mummified creature. Go above! With a rustling like the pages of an ancient book it moved—flung its arm over its eyes!

I'm afraid I may have screamed. But almost immediately I realized that the terror had been of my own postulation. Corpses do not move. This thing had moved—therefore it was not a corpse, and I had better get hold of myself unless I was determined to go batty.

It was revolting but necessary that I examine the thing. From its fingers thin, fine silver wires led into holes in the slab. I rolled it over, not heeding its terrible groans, and saw that a larger strand penetrated the neck, apparently in contact with its medulla oblongata. Presumably it was sick—this was a hospital. I rambled about cheerfully, scanning cryptic dials on the walls, wondering what would happen next, if anything.

There was a chair facing the wall; I turned it around and sat down.

"Greetings, unknown friend," said an effeminate voice.

"Greetings right back at you," said I.

"You have seated yourself in a chair; please be advised that you have set into motion a sound track that may be of interest to you."

The voice came from a panel in the wall that had lit up with opalescent effects.

"My name," said the panel, "is unimportant. You will probably wish to know first, assuming that this record is ever played, that there are duplicates artfully scattered throughout this city, so that whoever visits us will hear our story."

"Clever, aren't you?" I said sourly. "Suppose you stop fussing around and tell me what's going on around here."

"I am speaking," said the panel, "from the Fifth Century of Bickerstaff."

"Whatever that means," I said.

"Or, by primitive reckoning, 2700 A.D."

"Thanks."

"To explain, we must begin at the beginning. You may know that Bickerstaff was a poor Scotch engineer who went and discovered atomic power. I shall pass over his early struggles for recognition, merely stating that the process he invented was economical and efficient beyond anything similar in history.

"With the genius of Bickerstaff as a prod, humanity blossomed forth into its fullest greatness. Poetry and music, architecture and sculpture, letters and graphics became the principal occupations of mankind."

The panel coughed. "I myself," it said, modestly struggling with pride, "was a composer of no little renown in this city.

"However, there was one thing wrong with the

Bickerstaff Power Process. That is, as Bickerstaff was to mankind, so the element yttrium was to his process. It was what is known as a catalyst, a substance introduced into a reaction for the purpose of increasing the speed of the reaction."

I, a chemical engineer, listening to that elementary rot! I didn't walk away. Perhaps he was going to say something of importance.

"In normal reactions the catalyst is not changed either in quantity or in quality, since it takes no real part in the process. However, the Bickerstaff process subjected all matter involved to extraordinary heat, pressure, and bombardment, and so the supply of yttrium has steadily vanished.

"Possibly we should have earlier heeded the warnings of nature. It may be the fault of no one but ourselves that we have allowed our race to become soft and degenerate in the long era of plenty. Power, light, heat—for the asking. And then we faced twin terrors: shortage of yttrium—and the Martians."

Abruptly I sat straight. Martians! I didn't see any of them around.

"Our planetary neighbors," said the panel, "are hardly agreeable. It came as a distinct shock to us when their ships landed this year—my year, that is—as the bearers of a message.

"Flatly we were ordered: Get out or be crushed. We could have resisted, we could have built war-machines, but what was to power them? Our brain-men did what they could, but it was little enough.

"They warned us, did the Martians. They said that we were worthless, absolutely useless, and they deserved the planet more than we. They had been watching our planet for many years, they said, and we were unfit to own it.

"That is almost a quotation of what they said. Not a translation, either, for they spoke English and indeed all the languages of Earth perfectly. They had observed us so minutely as to learn our tongues!

"Opinion was divided as to the course that lay before us. There were those who claimed that by hoarding the minute supply of yttrium remaining to us we might be able to hold off the invaders when they should come. But while we were discussing the idea the supply was all consumed.

"Some declared themselves for absorption with the Martian race on its arrival. Simple laws of bio-genetics demonstrated effectively that such a procedure was likewise impossible.

"A very large group decided to wage guerilla warfare, studying the technique from Clausewitz's 'Theory and Practise.' Unfortunately, the sole remaining copy of this work crumbled into dust when it was removed from its vault.

"And then . . .

"A man named Selig Vissarion, a poet of Odessa, turned his faculties to the problem, and evolved a device to remove the agonies of waiting. Three months ago—my time, remember—he proclaimed it to all mankind.

"His device was—the Biosomniac. It so operates that the sleeper—the subject of the device, that is—is thrown into a deep slumber characterized by dreams of a pleasurable nature. And the slumber is one from which he will never, without outside interference, awake.

"The entire human race, as I speak, is now under the influence of the machine. All but me, and I am left only because there is no one to put me under. When I have done here—I shall shoot myself.

"For this is our tragedy: Now, when all our yttrium is gone, we have found a device to transmute metals. Now we could make all the yttrium we need, except that . . .

"*The device cannot be powered except by the destruction of the atom.*

"And so, unknown friend, farewell. You have heard our history. Remember it, and take warning.

Be warned of sloth, beware of greed. Farewell, my unknown friend."

And, with that little sermon, the shifting glow of the panel died and I sat bespelled. It was all a puzzle to me. If the Martians were coming, why hadn't they arrived? Or had they? At least I saw none about me.

I looked at the mummified figures that stretched in great rows the length of the chamber. These, then, were neither dead nor ill, but sleeping. Sleeping against the coming of the Martians. I thought. My chronology was fearfully confused. Could it be that the invaders from the red planet had not yet come, and that I was only a year or two after the human race had plunged itself into sleep? That must be it.

And all for the want of a little bit of yttrium!

Absently I inspected the appendages of the time-travelling belt. They were, for the most part, compact boxes labeled with the curt terminology of engineering. "Converter," said one. "Entropy gradient," said another. And a third bore the cryptic word, "Gadenolite." That baffled my chemical knowledge. Vaguely I remembered *something* I had done back in Housatonic with the stuff. It was a Scandinavian rare earth, as I remember, containing tratia, eunobia, and several oxides. And one of them, I slowly remembered—

Then I said it aloud, with dignity and precision: "One of the compounds present in this earth in large proportions is yttrium dioxide."

Yttrium dioxide? Why, that was—

Yttrium!

It was one of those things that was just too good to be true. Yttrium! Assuming that the Martians hadn't come yet, and that there really was a decent amount of the metal in the little box on my belt . . .

Quite the little heroine, I, I thought cheerfully, and strode to the nearest sleeper. "Excuse me," I said.

He groaned as the little reading lamp flashed on. "Excuse me," I said again.

He didn't move. Stern measures seemed to be called for. I shouted in his ear, "Wake up, you!" But he wouldn't.

I wandered among the sleepers, trying to arouse some, and failing in every case. It must be those little wires, I thought gaily as I bent over one of them.

I inspected the hand of the creature, and noted that the silvery filaments trailing from the fingers did not seem to be imbedded very deeply in the flesh. Taking a deep breath I twisted one of the wires between forefinger and thumb, and broke it with ease.

The creature groaned again, and—opened its eyes!

"Good morning," I said feebly.

It didn't answer me, but sat up and stared from terribly sunken pits for a full second. It uttered a little wailing cry. The eyes closed again, and the creature rolled from its slab, falling heavily to the floor. I felt for the pulse; there was none. Beyond doubt this sleeper slept no longer—I had killed him.

I walked away from the spot, realizing that my problem was not as simple as it might have been. A faint glow lit up the hall, and the lights above flashed out. The new radiance came through the walls of the building.

It must be morning, I thought. I had had a hard night, and a strange one. I pressed the "Slavies' ring" again, and took the revolving staircase down to the lobby.

The thing to do now was to find some way of awakening the sleepers without killing them. That meant study. Study meant books, books meant library. I walked out into the polished stone plaza and looked for libraries.

There was some fruitless wandering about and stumbling into several structures precisely similar to the one I had visited; finally down the vista of a broad, gleaming street I saw the deep-carven words, "Stape Books Place," on the pediment of a traditionally squat, classic building. I set off for it, and arrived too winded by the brisk walk to do anything more than throw myself into a chair.

A panel in the wall lit up and an effeminate voice began, "Greetings, unknown friend. You have seated yourself in a chair; please be advised— "

"Go to hell," I said shortly, rose, and left the panel to go through a door inscribed "Books of the Day."

It turned out to be a conventional reading room whose farther end was a maze of stacks and shelves. Light poured in through large windows, and I felt homesick for old Housatonic. If the place had been a little more dusty I'd never have known it from the Main Tech Library.

A volume I chose at random proved to be a work on anthropology: "A General Introduction to the Study of Decapilation Among the Tertiates of Gondwana as Contrasted with the Primates of Eurasia." I found one photograph—in color—of a hairless monkey, shuddered, and restored the volume.

The next book was "The Exagmination into the incamination for the resons of his Works in pregreSs," which also left me stranded. It appeared to be a critique of the middle work of one James Joyce, reprinted from the original edition of Paris, 1934 A.D.

I chucked the thing into a corner and rummaged among the piles of pamphlets that jammed a dozen shelves. "Rittenhouse's Necrology"—no. "Statistical Isolates Relating to Isolate Statisticals"—likewise no. "The Cognocrat Manifest"—I opened it and found it a description of a superstate which had yet to be created. "Construction and operation of the Biosomniac"—that was it!

I seated myself at one of the polished tables and read through the slim pamphlet rapidly once, then tore out some of its blank pages to take notes on. "The arrangement of the regulating dials is optional," I copied onto the paper scraps, and sketched the intricate system of Bowden wires that connected the bodies with the controls. That was as much of a clue as I could get from the little volume, but it indicated in its appendix more exhaustive works. I looked up "Vissarion," the first on the list.

"Monarch! may many moiling mockers make my master more malicious marry mate—"

it said. Mankind, artist to the last, had yet found time to compose an epic poem on the inventor of the Bio-somniac. I flung the sappy thing away and took down the next work on the list, "Chemistry of the Somniac." It was a sound treatise on the minute yet perceptible functionings of the subject under the influence of the Vissarion device. More notes and diagrams, collated with the information from the other book.

"The vitality of the sleeper is more profoundly affected by the operations of the Alphate dial . . . It is believed that the Somniac may be awakened by a suitable manipulation of the ego-flow so calculated as to stock the sleeper to survive a severing of the quasi-amniotic wiring system."

I rose and tucked the notes into my belt. That was enough for me! I'd have to experiment, and most likely make a few mistakes, but in a few hours men would be awake to grow hard and strong again after their long sleep, to pluck out their wires themselves, and to take my yttrium and with it build the needed war-machines against the Martians. No more sleep for Earth! And perhaps a new flowering of life when the crisis of the invaders was past?

"The compleat heroine—quite!" I chortled aloud as I passed through the door. I glanced at the glowing panel, but it glowed no longer—the unknown speaker

had said his piece and was done. Onward and outward to save the world, I thought.

"Excuse me," said a voice.

I spun around and saw a fishy individual staring at me through what seemed to be a small window.

"What are you doing awake?" I asked excitedly.

He laughed softly. "That, my dear young lady,
is just what I was about to ask you."

"Come out from behind that window," I said
nervously. "I can hardly see you."

"Don't be silly," he said sharply. "I'm quite a
few million miles away. I'm on Mars. In fact, I'm a
Martian."

I looked closer. He did seem sort of peculiar,
but hardly the bogeyman that his race had been
cracked up to be. "Then you will please tell me what
you want," I said. "I'm a busy woman with little time
to waste on Martians." Brave words. I knew it would
take him a while to get from Mars to where I was;
by that time I would have everyone awake and sting-
ing.

"Oh," he said casually. "I just thought you
might like a little chat. I suppose you're a time-traveler."

"Just that."

"I thought so. You're the fourth—no, the fifth—
this week. Funny how they always seem to hit on
this year. My name is Alfred, John Alfred."

"How do you do?" I said politely. "And I'm
Mable Evans of Colchester, Vermont. Year, 1940. But
why have you got a name like an Earthman?"

"We all have," he answered. "We copied it from
you Terrestrials. It's your major contribution to our
culture."

"I suppose so," I said bitterly. "Those jellyfish
didn't have much to offer anybody except poetry and
bad sculpture. I hardly know why I'm reviving them
and giving them the yttrium to fight you blokes
off."

He looked bored, as nearly as I could see. "Oh, have you some yttrium?"

"Yes."

"Much?"

"Enough for a start. Besides, I expect them to pick up and acquire some independence once they get through their brush-up with Mars. By the way—when will you invade?"

"We plan to *colonize*," he said, delicately emphasizing the word, "beginning about two years from now. It will take that long to get everything in shape to move."

"That's fine," I said enthusiastically. "We should have plenty of time to get ready, I think. What kind of weapons do you use? Death-rays?"

"Of course," said the Martian. "And heat rays, and molecular collapse rays, and disintegrator rays, and resistance rays—you just name it and we have it in stock, lady."

He was a little boastful. "Well," I said, "you just wait until we get a few factories going—then you'll see what high-speed, high-grade production can be. We'll have everything you've got—double."

"All this, of course," he said with a smug smile, "after you wake the sleepers and give them your yttrium?"

"Of course, Why shouldn't it be?"

"Oh, I was just asking. But I have an idea that you've made a fundamental error."

"Error, my neck," I said. "What do you mean?"

"Listen closely, please," he said. "Your machine—that is, your time-traveller—operates on the principle of similar circles, does it not?"

"I *seem* to remember that it does. So what?"

"So this, Miss Evans. You postulate that firstly the circumference of all circles equals infinity times zero. Am I right?"

That was approximately what Stephen had said, so I supposed that he was. "Right as rarebits," I said.

"Now, your further hypothesis is probably that

all circles are equal. And that equal distances traversed at equal speeds are traversed in equal times. Am I still right?"

"That seemed to be the idea."

"Very well." A smug smile broke over his fishy face. He continued. "Your theory works beautifully—but your machine—no."

I looked down at myself to see if I were there. I was.

"Explain that, please," I said. "Why doesn't the machine work?"

"For this reason. Infinity times zero does not equal *a* number. It equals *any* number. A definite number is represented by *x*; *any* number, *n*. See the difference? And so unequal circles are still unequal, and cannot be circumnavigated as of the same distance at the same speed in the same time. And your theory—is a fallacy."

He looked at me gloatingly before continuing. Then, slowly, "Your theory is fallacious. Ergo, your machine doesn't work. If your machine doesn't work, you couldn't have used it to get here. There is no other way for you to have gotten here. Therefore . . . *you are not here!* and so the projected *colonization* will proceed on schedule?"

And the light flashed in my head. Of course! that was what I had been trying to think of back in the house. The weakness in Trainer's logic!

Then I went *pouf* again, my eyes closed, and I thought to myself, "Since the machine didn't work and couldn't have worked, I didn't travel in time. So I must be back with Trainer."

I opened my eyes. I was.

"You moron," I snapped at him as he stood goggle-eyed, his hand on the wall socket. "Your machine doesn't work!"

He stared at me blankly. "You were gone. Where were you?"

"It seemed to be 2700 A.D.," I answered.

"How was it?" he inquired, reaching for a fresh flask of ethyl.

"Very, very silly. I'm glad the machine didn't work." He offered me a beaker and I drained it. "I'd hate to think that I'd really been there." I took off the belt and stretched my aching muscles.

"Do you know, Mable," he said, looking at me hard, "I think I'm going to like this town."

VACANT WORLD

This story was a three-way collaboration—Cyril, myself, and Dirk Wylie—and was originally published under Dirk's name. Dirk was a founding Futurian, and a long-time friend of mine. (We met as freshmen at Brooklyn Technical High School, when we were both twelve.) Like most fans and nearly all Futurians, Dirk wanted to be a professional writer. He had talent. He was good at a kind of science fiction nobody seems to write any more: quixotic adventure, I suppose you would call it; the kind of thing that Percival Christopher Wren invented with **Beau Geste***. In science fiction it exists, among others, in the stories of C. L. Moore, notably the Jirel of Joiry and Northwest Smith series. I think the chances are good that we might now be saying "in the stories of Dirk Wylie" if a war hadn't come along just as he was hitting his stride. Dirk enlisted early. Like Cyril, he served in the Battle of the Bulge and, like Cyril, he ultimately paid for it with his life. Neither was wounded by enemy fire. What Dirk did was injure his back in a G.I. truck. It began to mend, then worsened and turned into tuberculosis of the spine, and he died of it at the age of twenty-nine.*

I. Return from Venus

"Happy New Year," Marvin said bitterly.

"Shuddup!" growled Camp, trying to chuck a

weightless book at him. "Him" was the talking lizard, tentatively christened *petrosaurus parlante veneris*, and generally sworn at as Marvin. Camp sorely regretted the day he had ever taught the little creature to talk; now its jeering, strangely booming voice was never still. He would have stuffed it if he had had the courage to kill it first, but in many ways August Camp was a sensitive man.

Marvin silenced, except for his eternal, sarcastic chuckle, Camp turned again to his log book. "Final entry," he wrote. "September 17, 1997. Approximately one hundred thousand kilometers from Earth at the present time, 10:17:08 A.M. I shall set the robot pilot for Newark Landing Field, wavelength IP twelve, and the Third Venus Expedition will be over."

He locked the manuals and swung a cover over their multiple pins and contacts, and threw the switch that would put the ship under the guidance of the Newark beam. A space-sphere couldn't be landed easily—not, at least, without outside assistance. There were nearly one million factors too many, all of them interacting, which had vital bearing on the dynamics of the particular vessel trying to ease itself to the seared pave of the field.

At the Newark port there were monstrous machines that would shudder into action as soon as his flares were detected—computators which would grind out the formulae of his descent, using a strange, powerful mathematics all their own. No human mind could do that unaided, nor could Camp's ship accommodate even the immense charts that were the summarized and tabulated knowledge of the computators and the men who operated them.

Camp dragged himself along a line over to the small, unshuttered port and swiped a patch of frost from its center, using a patch of waste for the job; even at that his hand was chilled and numbed by the frightful cold of the thick glass. He stared through the port at the meager slice of Earth that he could see, old, half-forgotten memories crowding his brain,

and his muscles tensed at the thought of seeing people once more. The first thing he would do, he decided, would be to head for Manhattan and walk up
and down Broadway as long as he could.

No more loneliness. No more talking to oneself
or to a brainless lizard. . . .

Camp had started, not alone, but with two com-
panions. One had died on the trip out to Venus three
years ago, lost in space—that had been Manden—
and the other, Gellert, had disappeared from their
stockaded camp on the cloudy planet; for two years
Camp had been alone, doing the jobs of three men
and doing them remarkably well. It had been difficult, of course, but . . .

. . . it was not supposed to be a joy ride. And
things were just as tough, in a relative way, on Terra.
The cycle of murderous wars just completed had left
great, leprous areas of poisoned land scabbing the
Earth's surface. Oil pools were empty and coal beds
depleted; clean, fertile ground was at a minimum.
A new source of supply had to be found.

Camp was not the first of the interplanetary
travellers; in the late Sixties Soviet Russia had been
seized by a passion for exploration of the other
worlds. Most of their huge ships had failed in one
way or another, with appalling loss of life, but one
had managed to reach the moon. The period that
followed the next successful flights was one of feverish lunar exploration and even madder scram-
bling for concessions when it was found that the
moon was rich in the materials needed on Earth. As
might have been foreseen, this soon produced another war.

The conflict was of short duration, and men
once more looked to the stars. A new, more powerful
propellant had been developed during the war, and
using this fuel, an expedition managed to reach the
cloud-wrapped surface of Venus. A second expedition soon followed, and a third, of which Camp was
a member.

The results of Camp's investigations had exceeded his wildest hopes. Venus, while too young a world to have much (if any) coal or oil, was still rich in minerals and cellulose organisms; the industrial processes of Terra could easily be adapted to employ cellulose fuels. The ground was swampy, for the most part, and contained a high percentage of a sort of peat. That constituted the principal source of danger to potential colonists; a fire in a Venusian peat-bog would kindle a blaze that might sweep hundreds of square miles.

Then too, there wasn't a drop of drinkable water to be had on the planet. But with distilling apparatus, and fuel to be had for the mere digging of it, what problem was that?

Camp muttered in annoyance as he blotted the page he was working on, and he crumpled the sheet and tossed it into a corner. The slight motion lifted him from his seat and sent him drifting across the cluttered cabin. He cursed absently at the inconveniences of weightlessness, and hauled himself back to his former position. He looked up suddenly. There was something wrong!

"Oh, my God!" he gasped. His continued lack of weight meant that the sphere was still falling free, that for some reason Newark had not taken over control. He yanked the shell from the robot and peered intently at its intricacies; it was not in operation. Hastily he checked the device for faulty connections in any of its delicate grids, and turned away unsatisfied. As far as he could tell the receiver was in perfect condition.

Fifty thousand kilometers to fall . . .

Then the observatories had not seen his signals, rockets that exploded with a ground-shaking detonation. . . . But why not? Had another war begun in his absence, to make mysterious explosions a matter of slight notice? If he only had a radio. . . . Newark! *Newark!* Why don't you take over, Newark?

One thousand . . .

Should he unlock the manuals? Was he adept

enough to jockey the huge space-sphere to a safe landing? Perhpas he would gun the motors too much, to find himself a scant hundred meters from the surface with his tanks drained to the dregs. Or he might keep his jets open too long, and send a destructive backwash into his motors.

Newark! Where are you, Newark?

Nine hundred kilometers . . . a thin whistle keened through the ship as it plunged through the first fringes of atmosphere.

He unlocked the manuals and touched a switch. The grating beneath his feet quivered in sympathy with the awakened motors, and weight suddenly returned to him as the sphere's shrieking descent was checked by the powerful jets. He could see, from his place at the C-panel, almost all of North America, rapidly increasing in size as he watched. He shot a swift glance through another port. The sky was still black, but already more than half of the stars whose shifting configurations he had come to know were gone, their feeble emissions filtered out by the thin blanket of air which had been interposed.

He cut the jets, and again the ship fell free; this was by far the cheapest means of descent, in terms of fuel. He fired a short burst from a secondary jet to clear a slowly drifting lake of cirrus clouds far below, and the Great Lakes suddenly appeared beneath him. He closed a firing switch in sudden panic at the thought of making a submarine landing. The space-sphere had been designed to float, if necessary, but he had packed the buoyancy tanks with specimens and samples, depending on the Newark beam to land him safely.

The explosions of the steering-jet veered the sphere northward, well over the Canadian border, and the ship dropped again.

One hundred kilometers . . .

Like a dancer he tiptoed the vessel up and down, balancing it nicely and precisely on a blast, with a minimum of fuel expenditure, but dropping, always dropping, to the surface.

He snatched a hasty look at his altimeter. Only a couple of kilometers now, he thought, and prayed that the exactly-measured fuel would last out this moment of terrible need. He cut the jets again, knocked the legs from under the sphere, and fell in a last wild plunge.

He strained his eyes, staring intently at the altimeter—at the little spot of light creeping steadily toward a red line on the dial. They met! And Camp, his fingers quivering on a half score of firing-keys, kicked over a foot lever that opened the jets to their fullest capacity, and pressed the keys. The rockets flamed with their utmost, ravening power, and the smooth rush of the sphere jolted to a shuddering halt as it danced uncertainly at the tip of the column of hellfire.

He had stopped flat about one hundred meters from the ground, he observed. Swifter, then, than was compatible with absolute safety, he reduced the power of the blast, bit by tiny bit, and the sphere settled rapidly into the incandescent pit its fiery breath had dug. The jets coughed, picked up again ... and ceased altogether ... and the sphere settled easily into the impalpable ash of the pit.

II. Village of Silence

"Son of a ... !" Camp whispered, and in any other circumstances it would have been a curse. He lit a cigarette, watching the blue-gray smoke twist in slow, fantastic whorls across the cramped cabin, and wondered what he should do now. He absently released the lock that controlled the loading-port of the sphere, and watched idly as a small motor drove the heavy panel open to the air. A beam of sunlight, the first in three years, cut across the cabin, causing Marvin to chuckle with alarm. Camp tossed a black cloth over the reptile's cage. Marvin would keep, he thought, until it was discovered just what sunlight would do to the pallid little creature.

He finished his cigarette and flipped the butt through the open port. Years on another gravity and weeks in space had not spoiled his aim, he thought happily. Some things a man kept forever, once he'd acquired them.

Camp began to tap his foot impatiently. Then he began to count. Before he realized it ten minutes had passed, and still there were no high-pitched voices babbling outside, no white, excited faces peering through the port, no visitors to his crater to welcome him as befitting a returned hero.

Almost angrily he strode to the lip of the port's shelving door and vaulted to the top of the parapet of charred, powdered earth his landing had flung up. He had come down, he saw, near the shore of a fairly large body of water, a lake somewhere near Lake Superior, from what he'd been able to see during the descent. To his right was the water; to his left a concrete highway, and, a kilometer or two along the road, he saw the slick ferroconcrete structures of a town. But over all the country in his sight, there was not a single person to be seen, nor any sign of life.

He took a few steps toward the highway, stopped uncertainly, and returned to the spacesphere. He rummaged out a pack of cigarettes and matches, and stood for a moment balancing a heavy automatic in his palm. With a laugh at his own adolescent ideas he tossed the pistol back to its place and climbed once more from the crater. Something wriggled in his pocket.

"What the devil?" Camp asked of the empty air, and fished an eel-like Marvin from his white coverall.

"Women!" gloated Marvin, leering at Camp in idiot affection. "Lead me to 'em!"

Camp strode across the grass to the white streak of the highway. "You be good," he commanded, stuffing the lizard back into his pocket, "or I'll send you to bed without any sugar. We're going to call on the deacon."

The walk was a dismal and seemingly interminable keeping to the left of the concrete pavement, expecting any moment to be hailed by the klaxon of a five-decker bus roaring past. Camp plodded steadily toward the village, glad even for the slight company of Marvin.

"My God, but it's creepy," Camp said confusedly. There were not, he suddenly realized, even birds or animals to be seen, not an insect buzzing stridently. The town seemed asleep in the warm September sunshine, as quiet as a peaceful Sunday morning; here and there a gay-striped, orange-and-black awning flapped listlessly in the gentle breeze, and autos were parked in thin lines along the curbs.

But the awnings were torn and flapped by the wind's tugging fingers, and the bleaching cars stood on flat tires, rusting away where they were parked.

Camp strode along the main street of the village, searching, hunting, looking through the windows of the little specialty shops and the larger general stores, some of them empty and gaping like blind eyes where old-fashioned glass had shattered or fallen out. The stores were unlocked, all of them, indicating that whatever had befallen the populace had occurred during the daytime, and though Camp opened several doors, yet some undefined fear kept him from entering any of the shops. Dust was thick on the floors, eddied into drifts and strange designs by vagrant winds, yet in the food stores meats and fruits seemed solid and sweet enough beneath their vacuum-exhausted glass housings.

He hurried to the other side of the street, looking nervously over his shoulder as he went, to a print shop whose sign read, "The Meshuggeh Junction Advertiser." He poked tentatively at the door. Like all the others he had tried, it swung open beneath his touch, and its hinges protested loudly in the thick silence.

An ancient Goss power press was the chief feature of the press-room, dwarfing a single monotype, and racks of fonts and job presses for smaller work. And in the rolls of the Goss was a stream of paper midway between blank and finished page. It seemed to Camp that the operator of the Goss had had barely time enough to shut off the power before he—went away.

Camp forced himself to bend over and read the date of the paper in the press. It was the issue of the "Advertiser" for *Monday, May 22, 1995*...and today, the stunned Camp thought, is Wednesday, the seventeenth of September, 1997!

He feverishly scanned what little of the paper was made up, finding no clue to the nightmare he was experiencing. He stepped from the shop, at last, and stood blinking for a moment in the bright afternoon sunshine.

Then he heard the silence...what silence! Silence deep and unbroken, unending, terrifying...silence blanketing a world! He whirled suddenly and shouted, flinching as the echo bounced eerily back from the nearby hills. He went on down the street, looking around at every step. He felt that if he could turn quickly enough, he would see somebody peering stealthily over a window-sill or around a door. His hurried pace turned into a run.

"You're crazy, Camp," Marvin jeered from his pocket.

Camp found himself at the village docks. There were boats moored there, the gay-bannered cruisers and motor-yachts of vacationers who had been there for the spring fishing and camping when *it*—whatever unimaginable thing the single syllable implied—happened.

Only the larger and newer craft, those with the *duraloy* hulls so popular before Camp had left for another planet, were still afloat, and all of these, he soon discovered, needed repairs of one sort or another before they would run. He finally chose, after thorough inspection, a sturdy cabin cruiser. Its tanks were slopping-full of oil, but Camp wasn't quite sure how good this would be after its two-year ripening. He drained the tanks accordingly, and refilled them from sealed cans he had found.

He started the motors, grimacing as thick clouds of black smoke vomited from the twin exhausts and backfire popped sharply once or twice, indicating vital need of a tune-up.

He worked grimly and silently, the only sounds breaking the heavy quiet being the clicking of his tools and the strident buzz of a battery charger. Dimly apparent in the back of his mind was an awareness of inimically circling shadows, of a vague menace watching him as he worked, and he shivered uncontrollably.

At last it was too dark to continue the repairs. He straightened his aching back and tossed his wrench aside, wiping a gob of grease from his face with a bit of waste. He stepped into the darkness of the battery-room, a darkness relieved only by the spasmodic, cold, blue flickering spark of the charger. The door closed behind him.

Camp pried one eye open a terrific trifle and yawned. Halfway through the yawn he sat bolt-upright, his heart pounding against his ribs like a frightened steam hammer, and stared about the small, bare room.

"Well?" a jeering voice demanded, and Camp jumped. Memory returned to him with a rush.

Unwilling, in his unfamiliarity, to leave the batteries charging all night, he had turned off the charger; finding this couch in an adjoining room, the gas station had seemed as good a place as any to bed down for the night. And the voice? Marvin, of course.

He had but to connect a starter-wire or so and clean up the resultant mess in the motor-well of the cruiser, and carry a few cases of canned food aboard. A map he had found indicated that this was Lake Nipigon, in Ontario. Nipigon, he knew, connected with Lake Superior; once in the Great Lake he could head for Isle Royale and the town of Johns. Why he decided on his old summer home he didn't know, but familiar surroundings would be better than the terrifying stillness of this deserted, unknown village. He carefully steered through the maze of moored and awash craft before him, and once out in the lake, set the course for the mouth of the Nipigon River and left it up to the automatic steering gear....

The Nipigon River opened up into Lake Superior, and a large island—Isle Royale, by his map—loomed ahead, its bays offering comfortable harbor for his small craft. Camp paralleled its shore, searching for recognizable landmarks. At last he spotted the old, familiar buoy, and on the island, just over a clump of trees, the red roof of the hotel he had patronized in the old days. He put in to shore and tied up at the dock.

Quite suddenly Camp realized that he'd only a very sketchy breakfast and no lunch, and that he was hungry. He slung Marvin into a pocket again and said, "Come on, Marvin. We're off to see the wizard."

Marvin snuggled into a comfortable ball and sleepily corrected. "Lizard... petrosaurus parlante veneris..."

Camp soon found Broadway, the central avenue of the town, and wandered disconsolately past dusty alleys and snug little homes, all silent and dead. There was a cafeteria ahead, the only one the town boasted, and he listlessly entered, wondering vaguely if he should take one of the checks protruding from the dispenser.

He stepped behind the long counter, feeling singularly guilty, and saw plastic containers of milk stacked up by the score. He took one, broke the seal, and drained it. It was warm, of course, but pure, though the cream had formed a solid chunk at the top of the container; the sterile milk would not sour under any conditions or range of temperature once it had been imprisoned behind its translucent shell. A vacuum-trap container yielded a slice of cake, marbled with pink and green streaks, to his questing fingers. He bit into it and found it sound and firm, but powder-dry in his mouth. He set the slice down unfinished and coughed.

Repressing his resurgent panic with a distinct effort he walked slowly from the grave-quiet cafeteria—it was *too* spooky, that place which should have resounded with the clatter of knife and fork and plate quiet with the stillness of a deserted tomb, too spooky even for a ghost—and headed down the street to the public library. He had thought to find some hint, some clue to the disappearance of every living thing, but the library's doors were locked, and he walked on.

Far down the street something flickered . . . and again. Camp stared stupidly, waiting for a recurrence of the flash of motion. "Red," he said vaguely. "Red fabric." Had it been a banner of some sort, writhing under the caress of the afternoon breeze? No, he thought not. He quickened his pace. The flash had seemed to come from the door of a bookshop . . .

Cautiously Camp trotted to the other side of Broadway. The windows of the shop were smudged and dirty; he strained his eyes to peer past the streaky glass into the dark interior.

"Must have imagined it," he mumbled.

And then the door of the shop opened, and a girl stepped out to the bright sidewalk.

III. Girl Alone

Camp's eyes bulged dangerously. He knew her!

"Lois—Lois Temple!" he exclaimed, and ran across the street.

He grabbed her shoulders, shouting incoherent, near-hysterical questions at her, almost unsettled by his joy and relief at finding another human being. But she stared blankly at him, and yet—no! There was such a concentration of intense life in her eyes that for a moment he felt almost as though he had received a physical blow. Her eyes, for all that, were uniquely vacuous, and yet they seemed as penetrating as a powerful fog-light. Her lips worked slightly, as though she were reading an extraordinarily difficult passage in some obscurely written book, and Camp felt, as he later phrased it, as though someone were stirring his brains with a stick. Then her taut, white face relaxed, and she murmured, "August Camp!"

"Yeah," he babbled. "I just got back from Venus; came down on the other side of the border, by Lake Nipigon. But there was nobody there. There's nobody at all! Lois, what's happened?"

"August Camp," she said once more, as though to reassure herself. "One morning, two years ago, I woke up and found that everybody was gone. I've been alone ever since."

"Isn't anybody left?"

She shook her head, sending amber-colored ringlets tumbling about her pale face. "I've tried to work the telephones and a transmitting set I found," she said, "and there is never any answer."

He stared at her, suddenly noticing that she was dripping wet. "What the devil happened to you?" he demanded, indicating her soaked clothing.

"Fell in the lake."

Camp was puzzled by her costume. It was somewhat the same as the gown she had worn when last he'd seen her—but there was a subtle difference. It had been at a party then, the party for the Expedition members, and her dress had been fashionably modest. The lines of her present frock were the same, he saw, but the intent was somehow different. The dress was backless, and moreover, dipped sharply in front, baring more of her neck and slim, shapely shoulders than was strictly proper for the afternoon. The skirt apparently reached her ankles, but as she turned a trifle he saw that it was slit from hem to thigh.

"I landed in Canada," he repeated, "near Meshuggeh Junction. I was—scared—by the silence, and promoted myself a boat and buzzed over here to Johns. It's awfully odd that I should find the one person left on my first attempt."

The girl's attractive lips twitched in a smile.

"I don't understand it myself. Did you say that you came over by boat? There's not a single piece of machinery turning on the Earth today; all the generators have stopped. They've run out of fuel or broken down, or something."

Camp fished a flat case from the breastpocket of his coverall and popped a cigarette between his thin, crooked lips. "Odd," he commented. "My boat started easily enough after a minor overhaul, considering that the oil was all of two years old. Wonder the stuff didn't thicken or gum up."

"Your boat's a Diesel?" she asked irrelevantly.

Camp cast a covert glance at her. Her eyes were wide and staring; she looked far from well. There was a strange note to her low voice, a note of—effort, he thought. That, her odd, lonely survival, her inexplicable, though quite agreeable clothing—he decided to ask her. . . .

"Lois . . . I want you to tell me whatever you can about this."

"Yes?" she said, with white, even teeth flashing in a smile that he had remembered through all his three years of voluntary exile.

"I want you to tell me how you happened to keep alive—or here, rather—though everyone else has vanished. Tell me that, and how you managed to survive the past two years." This, he thought with some satisfaction, was a fair test.

He watched her face closely as she began to answer. Then—again that sensation of physical force, that feeling of mind-muddling probing that he'd experienced a few minutes before . . . and the girl slumped to the ground like a devitalized zombie.

"Damn me for a stupid, thoughtless ass!" Camp swore, and felt her pulse. She was alive, and her heartbeat was strong and regular; it seemed an ordinary faint, but he didn't dare take any chance.

There was the awful possibility that the only other human being on the Earth might die!

She had received a bad drenching when she had fallen into the lake, he thought; her skin was still wet. That, and the shock of their sudden encounter, must have taken heavy toll of her strength. He gathered her up in his strong arms—she was so like a little child!—and carried her to the boat.

As he set her down he thought vaguely that she must have lost weight. Her hair was a little longer, too, as he would have wished it to be. Altogether she was nearer to his ideal than she had been when last he saw her, and in no way had the certain privations of her solitude affected her beauty.

He placed her gently in one of the small bunks, drawing the blankets up around her chin, and set canned broth heating on the incredibly tiny electric stove. He had noticed, during the trip over, that the generator seemed to be out of kilter, and he took this opportunity of repairing it.

It was getting rather dark now, and working partly by touch, partly by the illumination of a droplight, he had jerry-rigged the cruiser's generator to operate satisfactorily. Fumbling a bit in the cramped space of the motor-well he reconnected the mechanism and started the motor. Tiny sparks inside the housing of the generator assured him that his work was serviceable, and he turned away satisfied.

He stiffened as he heard a little moan from Lois's bunk. She must be coming to, he thought. A full-grown scream yanked him bodily from the hatch, and he skidded madly into the cabin.

Lois was tossing feverishly in the narrow bunk, writhing in the nastiest convulsions Camp had ever seen. He grasped her wrist.

"There, there," he crooned soothingly, smoothing the damp hair back from her sweat-slicked face. Her eyes opened wide, and she stared agonizedly at him. Another raw scream ripped her throat, and she clawed wildly at Camp's restraining grip.

Insane or delirious, he thought. He muttered what he hoped to be calming words as he frantically rummaged through the lockers in search of a medicine kit, intending to give her a sedative. Looking back at her as her screams whispered away, he saw that her normally creamy skin was darkening.

"What the hell?" he whispered. His quick mind, accustomed to instantly analyzing the split-second phases of Venusian botany, tore the situation apart and reintegrated it satisfactorily. Her spasms had begun when he started the motors. Was it possible that the stale oil in the fuel tanks had suffered a deterioration causing it to emit poisonous fumes? With an exclamation he hurried to the controls and switched off both motors. Almost at once the girl's moans were stilled and her wild tossings ceased, with no more movement than an occasional twitch of relaxing muscles. Her tawny eyes closed, and her breathing again became regular and effortless.

If the motors were throwing off dangerous gases . . . Camp dragged a mattress and blankets from the other bunk and fixed a fairly comfortable bed on deck, on the windward side of the twin motors and out of range of any potential fumes.

Back in the cabin, he took Lois's wrist to check her pulse; she had fallen into a quiet, easy sleep. Pulse normal again, he thought, and thank God for that! But—her wrist was still wet! She'd had plenty of time to dry off since he had found her. Curiously he wiped away the film of moisture from her skin, and felt it again. Cold, rather, and not a little slimy. No—not slimy, he decided, but slippery . . . like a seal's smooth hide.

With a baffled shake of his blond head he picked the girl up and easily carried her up the short ladder to the deck. Gently he deposited her on the mattress and returned to his work.

The starter switch stared at him like a cold, unwinking, metallic eye. He petulantly stabbed the button. The motors purred again.

And again the air was torn by that shrill scream! One desperate leap pulled Camp over the hatch coaming to the deck. For a split-second too long he stared at an empty mattress—and out of the corner of his eye saw something slither over the side of the boat. He dashed to the rail and stared through gathering darkness into the water; there was nothing to be seen but a widening series of ripples....

The black night pressed closer upon him, and a chill wind sowed through the trees on the shore. But it was quiet—so very quiet! Then Marvin's raucous tones sounded, somewhere aboard the cruiser, pushing the heavy, menacing stillness aside and shaking Camp from his shocked immobility.

Something had reached aboard the cruiser—slipped aboard at a point not three meters from an alert, quick-nerved man whose existence had previously depended on his ability to scent danger... *something* was out there now, chuckling inhumanly as it lugged the girl off to whatever doom had overtaken the rest of the Earth's teeming millions....

He was sure that he had seen a bit of the bright red skirt that the girl had worn, and a slim arm crooked over the side of the boat... but something, he felt, was wrong, and he wished devoutly for the automatic he had left back at the space-sphere.

Had the thing really abducted Lois? Somehow he doubted that the girl had been seized against her will. So close together had been her body and the thing's blurred form, he thought that they might have been fervidly embracing each other.

IV. Twin Trouble

Camp stirred restlessly and awoke from a night filled with uneasy dreams. No solution of the preceding day's insane events had occurred to him while he slept, or if one had, he failed to recall it. Philosophically he turned on the stove and prepared for breakfast. He decided, after running an exploratory hand over his chin, to skip that day's shaving, and began to tumble through the cruiser's supplies, bringing to light a sealed tin of bacon. He opened it with the aid of a screwdriver, being unable to locate a can-opener, and carefully inhaled the aroma of the meat. He hadn't come several million kilometers to die of simple food poisoning.

A frying pan was placed on the stove, and the bacon arranged in careful rows on the hot surface. He smiled almost happily as the cabin became filled with the crisp breakfast smell, and set coffee to boil. He had found that given a good morning meal, a man could tackle almost anything with a fair hope of success.

His breakfast was set out soon, and he hungrily munched the crisp strips of bacon. Through a cabin port he could see Isle Royale and the town of Johns in the distance. He had cruised about a kilometer or so out before turning in, searching for any sign of whatever had taken Lois, recklessly exposing himself in the hope of drawing the thing from concealment. The past evening seemed like an unpleasant dream, until—

A shadow darkened his plate, and he looked up.

"You," he stated coldly, "are about the most irregular creature I've ever met."

"Nuts!" Marvin lipped, and scuttled to the protection of the leg of his master's coverall.

Lois smiled brightly, and sat down opposite the staring Camp. "Most men are irritable before breakfast," she said. "Finish your bacon, and maybe then you'll be in a better mood."

Camp obediently speared a chunk of bacon, looked distastefully at it, and put it down again.

"How did you get here?" he demanded. "And what the hell, if you'll pardon my language, happened to you last night?"

She gestured vaguely.

"Something grabbed me," she said. "Something

fishy grabbed me when I was only half conscious, and dragged me overboard."

"'Something fishy' is right!" Camp snorted. "For God's sake, what did the thing look like?"

"I couldn't describe it," Lois said, and shuddered. "It had arms, and it weaved through the water— "

"Where'd it take you?"

"On shore at Isle Royale, to a cove near Johns. When I came to I saw it watching me, and I ran for the lake and jumped in. It didn't follow me—no, I don't know why—and I swam back to the boat and climbed on . . . and here I am. Does that make sense, or bring the story up to date?"

"Um," Camp said thoughtfully. "I guess so." He scratched his stubbled chin, wishing he had shaved after all. He looked again at his plate of bacon and tinned bread. "Here," he said, climbing to his feet, "I'll fix up some of this for you."

"No," said the girl. "I don't want any."

Camp frowned. What was wrong with her? He knew that she hadn't eaten for hours—a whole day, at least.

"Nonsense," he said firmly. "You've got to eat something." He tossed some more bacon into the pan and turned the current high. In a moment or so the food was ready and sizzling. He slipped the strips into a plate and set it down before the girl.

"There," he said. "Stow that away and maybe we'll get the sparkle back in your eyes. Very nice eyes, too."

The girl looked wanly at the plate of food. "I really don't want any," she said faintly. "I'm afraid you won't be able to spare it."

Camp glowered at her. "With the supplies of a whole world to be looted? Of course I'll be able to spare it," he persisted. "And anyway, it's cooked already. On moral grounds alone you should eat it; the stuff'll be wasted otherwise. I don't think I could comfortably manage more bacon myself."

Lois smiled weakly, and stared blankly at the loaded plate. As though she were forcing herself to an unpleasant task she picked a bit of bacon and swallowed it.

"No," she said suddenly. "I don't want to— " and broke off. Her face was set in definite lines of disgust; the food seemed to have made her slightly ill.

The baffled Camp removed the plate. "Okay," he said apologetically. "I'm sorry if there's anything wrong. Don't you like bacon?"

"No," she replied, with evident relief. "Not bacon."

"Then how about a string of sausages? Rich and racy, ground from happy hogs," he suggested with ill-advised humor. Lois retched daintily.

"Not sausages," the girl answered, somewhat unevenly. "The thought of it makes me ill. I would like a drink of water, though." Camp poured a glass for her, and watched silently as she swallowed it in one quick gulp. "That was good," she smiled. "That took the edge off my appetite."

Camp blinked. "Oh?" he said. "But you can't live on water!"

Lois arched one thin eyebrow. "No? I can try."

And again something seemed to click in place inside the man's mind. The preposterous contradictions of the whole damned, fantastic set-up seemed to point to some huge, shadowy, indistinct conclusion far off in the distance—and, he thought, he feared for his sanity.

"Lois," he said firmly, "sit down." She obeyed, and he assumed a commanding posture above her. "Now," Camp went on, "what precisely is wrong with me or the world—or perhaps just you? I still don't know how you, of all the living things on Earth, survived whatever happened; I still don't know what it was that did happen; I don't know a single thing about your disappearance last night . . . and I don't think you'd tell me the truth anyway."

"But— " she began.

"None of that!" he snapped, and slammed his hand down hard on the tabletop. Marvin squeaked shrilly and scurried into Camp's pocket.

"If I've guessed right," Camp intoned, "you've got some ungodly peculiar friends!"

There was a faint scratching noise behind him. Camp whirled, his hard fists poised and ready for anything.

Ready for anything but what he saw. For it was Lois there in the cabin's doorway.

He shot one quick, unbelieving glance at the girl sitting quietly in the chair behind him, and then looked at her exact twin only two or three meters away. They were, he saw unbelievingly, alike in every detail.

The two girls stared at each other in obvious confusion. It was plainly apparent to Camp that something had gone wrong with the plans of one— or both.

"What the hell is this?" he growled helplessly.

There was no answer.

He strode to the cabin door and stood before it, blocking it with his broad shoulders. "Neither one of you two phonies gets out of here until I find out what's going on," he rasped. "You!" This to the second Lois. "Where'd you come from?"

"From—from Isle Royale," she faltered. "Something fishy grabbed me when I was only half— "

He stopped her with a choppy motion of one bronzed hand. "That's enough," he said curtly. He eyed the two girls angrily.

"I don't know what's going on, or what your game is," he said, "but I'm going to give you one chance to talk before I put the screws on. One chance . . . will you talk now, or shall I get tough?"

No answer, except an apprehensive stirring.

"Okay," he lipped. "I haven't forgotten what happened when I ran the generator last night. I'm going to turn it over now, and we'll see which one of you throws the first fit."

A quick glance assured him that the cabin's two

ports were too small to allow the passage of even the girl's slim bodies. He stepped outside, and slammed the door and bolted it.

As soon as he had started the generator he raced back to the cabin. He knew that blue sparks must now be chasing themselves around the brushes of the generator, and he watched the girls carefully.

And then . . . *both* girls collapsed in horrible, writhing convulsions!

Camp stared in horrified fascination at their frenzied, whipping contortions. Every theory of his was shot, now; he was certain that neither girl was Lois. But if neither one was the girl he knew—*what were they?*

Their struggles were pitiable, but Camp could be diamond-hard when the necessity arose. Grimly unheeding of their screams he waited for the next development. The discoloration he had seen last night spread simultaneously over the skins of the two sufferers, a rash that seemed to extend itself into a silky, dark-hued coating.

"My God!" he cried thinly. The girls were— melting—losing their forms! Slumping into ovoid, tapering creatures that flopped about the floor, each whipping eight short tentacles in open discomfort. Suddenly, then, he knew. These creatures—it had been one of them which he had seen slip over the side of his boat last night, not *carrying* an unconscious girl but *halfway transformed from human to monster!*

V. Restoration

"Gah!" Camp said feelingly. He tumbled backwards out of the suddenly cramped cabin and grabbed up the rifle. Marvin, in his pocket, protested sleepily at the sudden commotion.

A metallic click accompanied the introduction

of a cartridge into the chamber of the rifle, and Camp felt better. He peered cautiously into the comparative darkness of the cabin.

A clear, curiously gentle voice seemed to sound in his brain.

"Earthman," it said. "Turn off your motors. We will not harm you."

Camp thought it over for a second, and switched off the motors, though not letting his hand stray too far from the starter button.

"Who said that?" he demanded, suspiciously eyeing the two limply relaxed creatures.

One of them oozed forward a trifle. "That's far enough!" Camp warned hastily.

"I did," came that clear voice again.

"Yeah?" Camp said. His hand hovered indecisively over the starter switch. "Start at the beginning of everything and tell me all about it." Cradling the rifle in the crook of his elbow he fished a cigarette from his pocket and applied the flame of a small briquet to its tip. . . .

"The name of our race," the thing began, "would mean nothing to you. It is sufficient only to say that we have come from another dimensional plane coexistent with your Earth, bound in certain relationships with your world by natural laws.

"We have always been a quiet, peaceable people, previously ignorant of death, for the world from which we come does not know that terrible phenomenon. Our science had overcome that, had passed beyond the point in the histories of all worlds whereat the vibrations of the mind gain dominance over matter; by a very small expenditure of effort we can mould any mass to serve our needs."

Camp snorted blueish smoke. "Go on," he drawled amiably, settling the rifle into a more comfortable position. He felt an almost overwhelming desire to laugh. "Go on. I may as well tell you that you don't actually exist, that I'm only dreaming you, but go ahead anyway. What brought you to Earth, or shouldn't I ask that?"

The creature's soft, wistful eyes regarded him steadily. "From another world alien to us," it continued. "They were a race of conquerors, and to us were as horrible as we must seem to you. They had weapons, and they conducted a swift, merciless war upon us. Most of my people were killed, since we could do no such thing as taking the lives of our foes, even to save our race from total extinction."

The other alien being wriggled forward. When it "spoke," Camp was astounded to detect a difference of timber and expression in the tone of the telepathed words.

"So," the thing said, continuing the rather one-sided conversation, "we left our world. The handful—literally—of us that were left was rotated into this plane and onto this planet, whose existence the experiments of our scientists had led us to suspect. But ... our people could not live with yours. We are terrifically sensitive to certain types of electrical radiations, as you have seen, and the myriad power-operated machines which made things pleasant and comfortable for you would have meant our deaths."

"Um," remarked Camp, and slapped Marvin's sharp little teeth away from his thigh.

"I'm a lone cowhand," the small lizard announced, somewhat irrelevantly. Camp scowled.

"So?" he prompted. "What then?"

The thing hesitated, and looked at its companion.

Then, "There is a third plane parallel with our own and this one, but it is a bleak world of eternal gloom, lit only by terrifying sheets of radiation from random stars which dip over its surface. To both your race and mine it would normally be uninhabitable—in fact, we would be unable to survive there under any conditions—but it was thought that all the inhabitants of Earth, all living things, could be placed under suspended animation and rotated into this plane. They would come to no harm, and would know absolutely nothing of what had been done to them. In time we would awaken them and bring them back to their home; we know, you see, that in ten years or so, as you measure time, our enemies will have destroyed themselves."

Camp nodded slowly. "I see," he said thoughtfully. "You had a hell of a nerve, though, to do what you did, but I suppose you had some justification. I suppose, too, that I'm crazy, but I believe you. I'm willing to call the war off and play on your side."

"Thank you," the creatures said together.

"And as a friend," went on one of them, "we ask you not to use any equipment that would generate sparks or short radio waves if you can possibly help it. You've seen what it does to us."

Camp stowed the rifle in a corner where it would be out of the way, but not too unhandy in case of need. These disturbing creatures, with their seal-and-octopus bodies and quiet mental voices, were spooky enough, and while they might be on the level, he thought, still it was best to take no chances.

"Okay," he agreed, however. "Mind if I ask a favor in return? I'd rather you assumed human forms whenever you can, around me. It's a trifle disconcerting to find such lofty ideals and intellects in such—er—unusual—bodies."

The two creatures blurred and expanded swiftly. Again they were twin Lois Temples.

"Ah—no," Camp said hurriedly. "Could one of you change to some other person? I hate to be such a bother, really, but . . ."

One of the girls said, "Think of a person; we can imitate his form."

Camp searched his mind for friends, and smiled ruefully as he failed to correctly visualize a single person. When he looked up he gasped.

"Hugo!" he exclaimed. "Hugo Manden!"

"No," corrected the image. "His body idealized by you. I found this figure in the back of your mind, surrounded with much respect and sorrow. Who was Hugo Manden?"

"A rather close friend of mine," Camp explained. "He died in space, while we were bound for Venus." His thoughts rambled for a moment. There was something buzzing around in his brain . . .

"Yeah," Camp said suddenly. "Look, I got an idea! Why don't you people go to Venus? I just got back from there, and I know it's approximately the same as Earth. Certainly it offered me no particular inconvenience, and should present none to you. Then you can return my people to their homes, and everybody will be happy."

Manden's figure nodded gravely. "Splendid," he said simply.

Camp's jubilant expression suddenly faded, and he looked comically woeful and downcast.

"Yeah," he said dully. "Yeah, but I've only got one space-sphere, and that won't hold more than three or four of you. There was another ship at Newark, but that was dismantled for repairs or something before I left. Certainly I can't build one . . . can't you people do something about it? You did say that you could—ah—mould any mass to suit your needs."

"Not to that extent," Manden revised hastily. "By using the full power of all our minds, we might have, at one time; but now there are too few of us left. So few, I think, that one space-sphere will be quite large enough to carry us all. There are only twenty-seven of my race alive."

Camp tossed his cigarette butt into the water and watched it hiss into black extinction.

"Sure," he protested, "but even twenty-seven are too many to put in the ship. How are you going to manage it?"

Manden smiled. "Simple," he told Camp. "We can put all but three or four in a state of suspended animation for the length of the voyage."

But Camp was yet unsatisfied. "That's fine," he said. "That part's okay, but I just thought of something else. What, precisely, will you do about fuel?"

"No," Lois told him. "The sphere can be moved by telekinesis—mind-power. Three of us can do it."

Camp stood by a smooth-lined, waist-high machine, so-called by him though, as far as he could see, it had no moving parts whatsoever. At his side stood Manden, and shadowing the scene was the great, round bulk of the space-sphere.

"Not very big," commented Camp, indicating the odd machine. "How does the thing work?"

Manden stepped forward and inserted a fist-sized ball, its surface dotted with an intricate pattern of perforations, into a socket in the device.

"Its action is largely mental," he obligingly explained. "That small globe is a sort of matrix which has been impregnated with the proper thought patterns to set up the automatic operation."

"Stop right there," Camp said. "I can see that it'd be too deep for me to understand." He cast a sidelong glance at his companion. "I'm kind of going to miss you and your people. You've taught me a couple of tricks—besides that little knack of levitation—that wouldn't have been developed by our science for a heap of years."

Manden smiled slowly. "You, in return, have done a lot for us. You've given us a world where we can live in safety and perfect ease of mind. We would not have been happy here, Camp, knowing that we were mere usurpers."

"Yeah," Camp mumbled. "I guess you're right."

Manden, with Lois close behind him, hesitated a little. "Goodbye, Camp," they said simply, and as they hurried into the space-sphere Camp could see them slumping and blurring into their normal tentacled forms.

The great sphere stirred uneasily, rose swiftly toward the zenith in a long, graceful sweep. It was uncanny, Camp thought, to see that tons-heavy mass dance lightly skyward unaided by the ravening, fiendishly hot rocket blasts. He sat down to wait.

After a space of time, about five cigarettes later, he became aware of a growing tension in the air. The light breeze which had been playing with his hair as he sat there had died away, and the hot and oppressive atmosphere was unnaturally still. He shuffled his feet uneasily.

The sky had darkened, and now bloated clouds, like the swollen bellies of poisoned alley cats, scudded past in a frightened cavalcade. The wind, too, had picked up again, and wailed through the nearby trees like a mournful banshee.

Each individual hair on his body was standing erect, now, vitalized by the tension in the struggling, saturated atmosphere, and breathing was strangely difficult.

He threw himself flat on the quivering ground, and felt easier.

The machine that had been left was fairly blazing now, glowing angrily through its mantle of flame. Little whorls and specks of phosphorescence appeared, dancing like fireflies, danced and grew, solidifying as they grew. The explosion of the thunder expanded to the destruction of worlds, and the little specks of light increased in size.

"People!" Camp muttered thickly. And people they were, and all the living things of Earth with them, replaced to the millimeter in the spots from which they had been so summarily plucked by a refugee race.

Camp began to wonder how he would explain the loss of the space-sphere.

BEST FRIEND

Like most of the earliest Futurian stories, "Best Friend" was written to fill a hole in one of the magazines I was editing. I think it was in Edwin Balmer and Philip Wylie's **After Worlds Collide** *that I had, years before, read a throwaway line about a vanished alien race whose pets had been as intelligent as modern human beings. I had wanted to explore that further, from the point of view of the pets; Cyril agreed, and "Best Friend" was the result.*

Moray smoothed his whiskers with one hand as he pressed down on the accelerator and swung easily into the top speed lane. Snapping the toggle into a constant eighty-per, he lit a meat-flavored cigarette and replaced the small, darkly warm bar of metal in its socket. He hummed absently to himself. Nothing to do after you were in your right lane—not like flying. He turned on the radio.

"—by Yahnn Bastiën Bock," said the voice. Moray listened; he didn't know the name.

Then there breathed into the speeding little car the sweetly chilly intervals of a flute-stop. Moray smiled. He liked a simple melody. The music ascended and descended like the fiery speck on an oscillograph field; slowed almost to stopping, and then the melody ended. Why, Moray wondered plaintively, couldn't all music be like that? Simple and clear, without confusing by-play. The melody rose again, with a running mate in the oboe register, and like a ceremonial dance of old days they intertwined and separated, the silvery flute-song and the woody nasal of the oboe. The driver of the little car grew agitated. Suddenly, with a crash, diapasons and clarions burst into the tonal minuet and circled heavily about the principals.

Moray started and snapped off the radio. Try as he would, he never could get used to the Masters' music, and he had never known one of his people who could. He stared out of the window and stroked his whiskers again, forcing his thoughts into less upsetting channels.

A staccato buzz sounded from the dashboard. Moray looked at the road-signs and swung into a lower speed-lane, and then into another. He looped around a ramp intersection and drove into a side-street, pulling up before a huge apartment dwelling.

Moray climbed out into the strip of fuzzy pavement that extended to the lobby of the building. He had to wait a few moments for one of the elevators to discharge its burden; then he got in and pressed the button that would take him to Floor L, where lived Birch, whom he greatly wanted to marry.

The elevator door curled back and he stepped out into the foyer. He quickly glanced at himself in a long pier glass in the hall, flicked some dust from his jacket. He advanced to the door of Birch's apartment and grinned into the photo-eye until her voice invited him in.

Moray cast a glance about the room as he entered. Birch was nowhere to be seen, so he sat down patiently on a low couch and picked up a magazine. It was lying opened to a story called "The Feline Foe."

"Fantastic," he muttered. All about an invading planetoid from interstellar space inhabited by cat-people. He felt his skin crawl at the thought, and actually growled deep in his throat. The illustrations were terrifyingly real—in natural color, printed in three-ply engravings. Each line was a tiny ridge, so that when you moved your head from side to side the figures moved and quivered, simulating life. One was a female much like Birch, threatened by one of the felines. The caption said, "'Now,' snarled the creature, 'we shall see who will be Master!'"

Moray closed the magazine and put it aside. "Birch!" he called protestingly.

In answer she came through a sliding door and smiled at him. "Sorry I kept you waiting," she said.

"That's all right," said Moray. "I was looking at this thing." He held up the magazine.

Birch smiled again. "Well, happy birthday!" she cried. "I didn't forget. How does it feel to be thirteen years old?"

"Awful. Joints creaking, hair coming out in patches, and all." Moray was joking; he had never felt better, and thirteen was the prime of life to his race. "Birch," he said suddenly. "Since I am of age, and you and I have been friends for a long time—"

"Not just now, Moray," she said swiftly. "We'll miss your show. Look at the time!"

"All right," he said, leaning back and allowing her to flip on the telescreen. "But remember, Birch— I have something to say to you later." She smiled at him and sat back into the circle of his arm as the screen commenced to flash with color.

The view was of a stage, upon which was an elaborately robed juggler. He bowed and rapidly, to a muttering accompaniment of drums, began to toss discs into the air. Then, when he had a dozen spinning and flashing in the scarlet light, two artists stepped forward and juggled spheres of a contrasting color, and then two more with conventional Indian clubs, and yet two more with open-necked bottles of fluid.

The drums rolled. "Hup!" shouted the master-juggler, and pandemonium broke loose upon the stage, the artists changing and interchanging, hurling a wild confusion of projectiles at each others' heads, always recovering and keeping the flashing baubles in the air. "Hup!" shouted the chief again, and as if by magic the projectiles returned to the hands of the jugglers. Balancing them on elbows and heads they bowed precariously, responding to the radioed yelps of applause from the invisible audience.

"They're wonderful!" exclaimed Birch, her soft eyes sparkling.

"Passably good," agreed Moray, secretly delighted that his suggested entertainment was a success from the start.

Next on the bill was a young male singer, who advanced and bowed with a flutter of soulful eyelids. His song was without words, as was usual among Moray's people. As the incredible head-tones rose without breaking, he squirmed ecstatically in his seat, remembering the real pain he had felt earlier in the night, listening to the strange, confusing music of the Masters.

Moray was in ecstasy, but there was a flaw in his ecstasy. Though he was listening with all his soul to the music, yet under the music some little insistent call for attention was coming through. Something very important, not repeated. He tried to brush it aside ...

Birch nudged him sharply, a little light that you might have called horror in her eyes. "Moray, your call! Didn't you hear it?"

Moray snatched from a pocket the little receiving set his people always carried with them. Suddenly, and unmuffled this time, shrilled the attention-demanding musical note. Moray leaped up with haste ...

But he hesitated. He was undecided—incredibly so. "I don't want to go," he said slowly to Birch, astonishment at himself in every word.

The horror in Birch's eyes was large now. "Don't want to! Moray! It's your Master!"

"But it isn't—well, fair," he complained. "He couldn't have found out that I was with you tonight. Maybe he does know it. And if he had the heart to investigate he would know that—that— " Moray swallowed convulsively. "That you're more important to me than even he is!" he finished rapidly.

"Don't say that!" she cried, agitated. "It's like a crime! Moray—you'd better go."

"All right," he said sullenly, catching up his cape. And he had known all along that he would go. "You stay here and finish the show. I can get to the roof alone."

Moray stepped from the apartment into a waiting elevator and shot up to the top of the building. "I need a fast plane," he said to an attendant. "Master's call." A speedlined ship was immediately trundled out before him; he got in and the vessel leaped into the air.

One hundred thousand years of forced evolution had done strange things to the canine family. Artificial mutations, rigorous selection, all the tricks and skills of the animal breeder had created a super-dog. Moray was about four feet tall, but no dwarf to his surroundings, for all the world was built to that scale. He stood on his hind legs, for the buried thigh-joint had been extruded by electronic surgery, and his five fingers were long and tapering, with beautifully formed claws capable of the finest artisanry.

And Moray's face was no more canine than your face is simian. All taken in all, he would have been a peculiar but not a fantastic figure could he have walked out into a city of the Twentieth Century. He might easily have been taken for nothing stranger than a dwarf.

Indeed, the hundred thousand years had done more to the Masters than to their dogs. As had been anticipated, the brain had grown and the body shrunk, and there had been a strong tendency toward increased myopia and shrinkage of the distance between the eyes. Of the thousands of sports born to the Masters who had volunteered for genetic experimentation, an indicative minority had been born with a single, unfocussable great eye over a sunken nosebridge, showing a probable future line of development.

The Masters labored no longer; that was for the dog people and more often for the automatic machines. Experimental research, even, was carried on by the companion race, the Masters merely collating the tabulated results, and deducing from and theorizing upon them.

Humankind was visibly growing content with less in every way. The first luxury they had relinquished had been gregariousness. For long generations men had not met for the joy of meeting. There was no such thing as an infringement on the rights of others; a sort of telepathy adjusted all disputes.

Moray's plane roared over the Andes, guided by inflexible directives. A warning sounded in his half-attentive ears; with a start he took over the controls of the craft. Below him, high on the peak of an extinct volcano, he saw the square white block which housed his Master. Despite his resentment at being snatched away from Birch he felt a thrill of excitement at the sensed proximity of his guiding intelligence.

He swung the plane down and grooved it neatly in a landing notch which automatically, as he stepped out, swung round on silent pivots and headed the plane ready for departure.

Moray entered through a door that rolled aside as he approached. His nostrils flared. Almost at the threshold of scent he could feel the emanations of his Master. Moray entered the long, hot corridor that led to this Master's living quarters, and paused before a chrome-steel door.

In a few seconds the door opened, silently, and Moray entered a dark room, his face twitching with an exciting presence. He peered through the gloom, acutely aware of the hot, moist atmosphere of the chamber. And he saw his Master—tiny, shrivelled, quite naked, his bulging skull supported by the high back of the chair.

Moray advanced slowly and stood before the seated human. Without opening his eyes, the Master spoke in a slow, thin voice.

"Moray, this is your birthday." There was no emphasis on one word more than another; the tone was that of a deaf man.

"Yes, Master," said Moray. "A—friend and I

were celebrating it when you called. I came as quickly as possible."

The voice piped out again, "I have something for you, Moray. A present." The eyes opened for the first time, and one of the Master's hands gripped spasmodically a sort of lever in his chair. The eyes did not see Moray, they were staring straight ahead; but there was a shallow crease to the ends of his lips that might have been an atavistic muscle's attempt at a smile. A panel swung open in the wall, and there rolled out a broad, flat dolly bearing an ancient and thoroughly rotted chest. Through the cracks in the wood there was seen a yellowish gleam of ancient paper.

The Master continued speaking, though with evidence of a strain. Direct oral conversation told on the clairvoyant, accustomed to the short cuts of telepathy. "These are the biographies of the lives of the North American presidents. When you were very young—perhaps you do not remember—you expressed curiosity about them. I made arrangements then to allow you to research the next important find of source-material on the subject. This is it. It was discovered six months ago, and I have saved it for your birthday."

There was a long silence, and Moray picked up one of the books. It had been treated with preservatives, he noted, and was quite ready for work. He glanced at a title page unenthusiastically. What had interested him in his childhood was boring in full maturity.

"Are you ready to begin now?" whispered the human.

Moray hesitated. The strange confusion that he had felt was growing in him again, wordlessly, like a protesting howl. "Excuse me, please," he stammered, stepping back a pace.

The Master bent a look of mild surprise upon him.

"I am sorry. I—I don't wish to do this work." Moray forced himself to keep his eyes on the Master.

There was a quick grimace on the face of the human, who had closed his eyes and was slumped against the back of the chair. His sunken chin twitched and fell open.

The Master did not answer Moray for a long minute. Then his eyes flicked open, he sat erect again, and he said, "Leave me."

And then he stared off into space and took no further notice of Moray.

"Please," said Moray hastily. "Don't misunderstand, I want very much to read those books. I have wanted to all my life. But I— " He stopped talking. Very obviously, the Master had eliminated Moray from his mind. Just as Moray himself, having had a cinder in his eyes, would drop from his mind the memory of the brief pain.

Moray turned and walked through the door. "Please," he repeated softly to himself, then growled in disgust. As he stepped into the plane once more he blinked rapidly. In the hundred thousand years of evolution dogs had learned to weep.

Moray, looking ill, slumped deeper into the pneumatic couch's depths. Birch looked at him with concern in her warm eyes. "Moray," she said worriedly, "when did you sleep last?"

"It doesn't matter," he said emptily. "I've been seeing the town."

"Can I give you something to eat?"

"No," said Moray. With a trace of guilt he took a little bottle from his pocket and gulped down a couple of white pills. "I'm not hungry. And this is more fun."

"It's up to you," she said. There was a long silence, and Moray picked up sheets of paper that were lying on a table at his elbow. "Assignments as of Wednesday," he read, and then put down the sheaf, rubbing his eyes with a tired motion. "Are you doing any work now?" he asked.

Birch smiled happily. "Oh, yes," she said. "My master wants some statistics collated. All about concrete pouring. It's very important work, and I finished it a week ahead of time."

Moray hesitated, then, as though he didn't care, asked: "How are you and your Master getting along?"

"Very well indeed. She called me yesterday to see if I needed an extension of time for the collation. She was very pleased to find I'd finished it already."

"You're lucky," said Moray shortly. And inside himself, bursting with grief, he wondered what was wrong between his own Master and himself. Three weeks; not a single call. It was dreadful. "Oh, Birch, I think I'm going mad!" he cried.

He saw that she was about to try to soothe him. "Don't interrupt," he said. "The last time I saw my Master I—made him unhappy. I was sure he would want me again in a few days, but he seems to have abandoned me completely. Birch, does that ever happen?"

She looked frightened. The thought was appalling. "Maybe," she said hastily. "I don't know. But he wouldn't do that to you, Moray. You're too clever. Why, he needs you just as much as you need him!"

Moray sighed and stared blankly. "I wish I could believe that." He took out the little pill-bottle again, but Birch laid a hand on his.

"Don't take any more, please, Moray," she whispered, trying desperately to ease his sorrow. "Moray—a while ago you wanted to ask me something. Will you ask me now?"

"I wanted to ask you to marry me—is that what you mean?"

"Yes. To both questions, Moray. I will."

He laughed harshly. "Me! How can you marry me? For all I know I've lost my Master. If I have, I—I'm no longer a person. You don't know what it's like, Birch, losing half your mind, and your will, and all the ambition you ever had. I'm no good now, Birch." He rose suddenly and paced up and down the floor. "You *can't* marry me!" he burst out. "I think I'll be insane within a week! I'm going now. Maybe you'd better forget you ever knew me." He slammed out of the room and raced down the stairs, not waiting for an elevator.

The streetlights were out; it was the hour before dawn. Obeying a vagrant impulse, he boarded a moving strip of sidewalk and was carried slowly out to one of the suburbs of the metropolis. At the end of the line, where the strip turned back on itself and began the long journey back to Central Square, he got off and walked into the half-cultivated land.

He had often wondered—fearfully—of the fate of those of his people who had been abandoned by their Masters. Where did they go? Into the outlands, as he was?

He stared at the darkness of the trees and shrubs, suddenly realizing that he had never known the dark before. Wherever his people had gone there had been light—light in the streets, light in their cars and planes, light even at night when they slept.

He felt the hair on his head prickle and rise. How did one go wild? he wondered confusedly. Took off their clothes, he supposed.

He felt in his pockets and drew out, one by one, the symbols of civilization. A few slot-machine tokens, with which one got the little white pills. Jingling keys to his home, office, car, locker, and closet. Wallet of flexible steel, containing all his personal records. A full bottle of the pills—and another, nearly empty.

Mechanically he swallowed two tablets of the drug and threw the bottle away. A little plastic case... and as he stared at it, a diamond-hard lump in his throat, a fine, thin whistle shrilled from its depths.

Master's call! He was wanted!

Moray climbed from the plane under the frowning Andes and almost floated into the corridor of his Master's dwelling. The oppressive heat smote him in the face, but he was near laughing for joy when he opened the door and saw his Master sitting naked in the gloom.

"You are slow, Moray," said the Master, without inflection

Moray experienced a sudden chill. He had not expected this. Confusedly he had pictured a warm reconciliation, but there was no mistaking the tone of the Master's voice. Moray felt very tired and discouraged. "Yes," he said. "You called me when I was out at the fields."

The Master did not frown, nor did he smile. Moray knew these moods of the cold, bleak intellect that gave him the greater part of his own intelligence and personality. Yet there was no greater tragedy in the world of his people than to be deserted—or, rather to lose rapport with this intelligence. It was not insanity, and yet it was worse.

"Moray," said the Master, "you are a most competent laboratory technician. And you have an ability for archaeology. You are assigned to a task which involves both these divisions. I wish you to investigate the researches of Carter Hawkes, time, about the Fifteenth Century Anno Cubriensis. Determine his conclusions and develop, on them, a complete solution to what he attempted to resolve."

"Yes," said Moray dully. Normally he would have been elated at the thought that he had been chosen, and he consciously realized that it was his duty to be elated, but the chilly voice of his conscience told him that this was no affectionate assignment, but merely the use of a capable tool.

"What is the purpose of this research?" he asked formally, his voice husky with fatigue and indulgence in the stimulant drug.

"It is of great importance. The researches of Hawkes, as you know, were concerned with explosives. It was his barbarous intention to develop an explosive of such potency that one charge would be capable of destroying an enemy nation. Hawkes, of course, died before his ambition was realized, but we have historical evidence that he was on the right track."

"Chief among which," interrupted Moray—deferentially—"is the manner of his death."

There was no approval in the Master's voice as he answered, "You know of the explosion in which he perished. Now, at this moment, the world is faced with a crisis more terrible than any ancient war could have been. It involves a shifting of the continental blocks of North America. The world now needs the Hawkes explosive, to provide the power for restabilizing the continent. All evidence has been assembled for your examination in the workroom. Speed is essential if catastrophe is to be averted."

Moray was appalled. The fate of a continent in his hands! "I shall do my best," he said nervelessly, and walked from the room.

Moray straightened his aching body and turned on the lights. He set the last of a string of symbols down on paper and leaned back to stare at them. The formula—complete!

Moray was convinced that he had the right answer, through the lightning-like short cuts of reasoning, which humans called "canine intuition." Moray might have felt pride in that ability—but, he realized, it was a mirage. The consecutivity of thought of the Masters—not Moray nor any of his people could really concentrate on a single line of reasoning for more than a few seconds. In the synthesis of thought Moray's people were superb. In its analysis . . .

A check-up on the formula was essential. Repeating the formula aloud, Moray's hands grasped half a dozen ingredients from the shelves of the lab, and precisely compounded them in the field of a micro-inspection device. Actually, Moray was dealing with units measured in single molecules, and yet his touch was as sure as though he were handling beakers-full.

Finally titrated, the infinitesimal compound was set over a cherry-red electric grid to complete its chain of reactions and dry. Then it would explode, Moray realized—assuming he had the formula correct. But, with such a tiny quantity, what would be the difference?

Perhaps—at utmost—the room would be wrecked. But there was no time to take the stuff to the firing-chambers that were suspended high over the crater of the extinct volcano on flexible steel masts, bent and supported to handle almost any shock.

Moray swallowed two more pellets of the drug. He had to wait for its effect upon him, now, but he dared not take a larger dose.

He strode from the room, putting the formula in his pocket.

Wandering aimlessly through the building, he was suddenly assailed by the hot, wet aura of his Master. He paused, then nudged the door open a trifle and peered longingly within.

The Master was engaged in solitary clairvoyance, his head sagging down on his scrawny chest, veins and muscles visibly pulsing. Even in the utter darkness of his room, he was visible by a thin blue light that exuded from the points and projections of his body to flow about the entire skin.

The Master was utterly unconscious of the presence of his servant. Though Moray was not a child or a fool, he stemmed directly from the beautiful, intelligent creatures that used to hunt and play with men, and he could not stand up to the fierce tide of intellect that flowed in that room. With a smothered sound he turned, about to leave.

Then Moray heard a noise—quiet and almost restful at first, like a swarm of bees passing overhead. And then it rumbled into a mighty crash that made the elastic construction of the Master's house quiver as though stricken.

Suddenly he realized—the Hawkes explosive! It had worked! He looked at his Master, to see the blue glare fade as though it were being reabsorbed into his body. As the last of it vanished, lights glowed on around the room, bringing it to its accustomed shadowy twilight. The Master's head lifted.

"Moray," he whispered tensely. "Was that the explosive?"

A thin little ripple of delight surged along Moray's spine. He could both be blown to splintered atoms in the explosion, and the continent they were trying to save along with them—he didn't care! His Master had spoken to him!

He knew what he had to do. With a little growl that was meant to say, "Pardon!" he raced to the Master's side, picked him up and flung him over a shoulder—gently. They had to get out of the building, for it might yet topple on them.

Moray tottered to the door, bent under the double burden; pushed it open and stepped into the corridor. The Master couldn't walk, so Moray had to walk for him. They made slow progress along the interminable hall, but finally they were in the open. Moray set his burden down, the gangling head swaying, and—

Felt unutterably, incontrovertibly idiotic! For the air was still and placid; and the building stood firm as a rock; and the only mark of the Hawkes explosive was a gaping mouth of a pit where the laboratory had been. Idiot! Not to have remembered that the Hawkes would expend its force *downward*!

Moray peered shamefacedly at his Master. Yet there was some consolation for him, because there was the skeleton of a smile on the Master's face. Clearly he had understood Moray's motives, and . . . perhaps Moray's life need not finally be blighted.

For a long second they stood there looking into each other's eyes. Then the Master said, gently, "Carry me to the plane."

Not stopping to ask why, Moray picked him up once more and strode buoyantly to the waiting ship. Letting the Master down gently at the plane's door, he helped him in, got in himself, and took his place at the controls.

"Where shall we go?" he asked.

The Master smiled that ghost of a smile again,

but Moray could detect a faint apprehension in his expression, too. "Up, Moray," he whispered. "Straight up. You see, Moray, these mountains are volcanic. And they're not quite extinct. We must go away now, up into the air."

Moray's reflexes were faster than an electron-stream as he whipped around to the knobs and levers that sent the little ship tearing up into the atmosphere. A mile and a half in the sky, he flipped the bar that caused the ship to hover, turned to regard the scene below.

The Master had been right! The explosion had pinked the volcano, and the volcano was erupting in retaliation—a hot curl of lava was snaking into the atmosphere now, seemingly a pseudopod reaching to bring them down. But it was thrown up only a few hundred feet; then the lava flow stopped; cataclysmic thunderings were heard and vast boulders were hurled into the sky. It was lucky they'd got away, thought Moray as he watched the ground beneath quiver and shake; and luckier that no other person had been around, for the ship could carry but two.

And as he stared, fascinated, at the turmoil below, he felt a light, soft touch on his arm. It was the Master—the first time in all Moray's life when the Master had touched him to draw attention, Moray suddenly knew, and rejoiced—he had found his Master again!

"Let us go on, Moray," whispered the Master. "We have found that the explosive will work. Our job, just now, is done."

And as Moray worked the controls that hurled the ship ahead, toward a new home for his Master and toward Birch for himself, he knew that the wings of the ship were of no value at all. Tear them off! he thought, and throw them away? His heart was light enough to bear a world!

BEFORE THE UNIVERSE

"Before the Universe" was the first story Cyril and I published in collaboration. I published it myself, and watched the reader mail with considerable apprehension when the story hit the stands; we weren't very sure of ourselves. But the response was good. That was all we needed. We sat right down and wrote a sequel, "Nova Midplane," and then a third story in the series, "The Extrapolated Dimwit."

Unfortunately, by the time we came to the third story we discovered we were running out of things to say about our characters, and so we had to have help. In the Futurian way, we solved the problem by inviting in a third collaborator, Robert W. Lowndes, better known then as "Doc."

Lowndes had been a fan as long as any of us, but mostly by correspondence. It was the time of the Great Depression. Most of us were young enough to be sheltered by our families from the harsher aspects of that long deep sickness of the thirties, but Lowndes was all by himself in the world. He had to earn a living any way he could, and one of the ways was by working in a hospital in Connecticut. (Whence the "Doc.") We knew each other almost entirely by correspondence for several years, during which time I remember that he introduced me to J. K. Huysmans and I introduced him to J. B. Cabell (we didn't only read SF, you know), before things healed enough for him to visit, then move to, New York City. He became a resident of the primitive Futurian communes (dull, drugless, all-

male pads that they were) pursued his writing, ulti-
mately achieved every fan's dearest dream by get-
*ting a job as a professional editor (**Future Fiction,***
***Science Fiction Quarterly** and others) and has con-*
tinued as one ever since. "The Extrapolated Dimwit"
was first published in one of his magazines.

I. The Nobel Prize Twins

Jocelyn Earle was listening closely to her employer's
instructions. That was one of the things about Jocelyn; she always listened closely, even if she paid
no attention to suggestions once she stopped listening and started doing. He was telling her how to get
the story he wanted for the *Helio;* he knew she would
get the story her own way, but he told her anyway.
The important thing was, she would get the story.

"Do you know anything at all about Clair and
Gaynor?" he asked.

"No," she said.

"Well, you're the only one in the world who
doesn't. Don't you ever read the papers?" She shook
her head. He sighed and went on. "They are the Nobel Prize winners for the last half-dozen years.
They're the ones who wiped out cancer, made possible the beam-transmission of power, created about·
fifty new alloys that have revolutionized industry,
and originated the molecular-stress theory which is
the cornerstone of the new physics.

"Gaynor is the kid of the pair. He's the one that
never went to grade school, completed high school
in eighteen months, and had a Ph.D. by the time he
was fifteen. A child prodigy. Unlike most of those,
he never burnt out. He's still going stronger than
ever.

"Clair is the older and not quite so bright. He
was almost old enough to vote by the time he brought
out his thesis on Elementary Arithmetic (Advanced),
which is a little bit harder to master than vector analysis. But, as I say, he's older than Gaynor, and he's

had a chance to learn a lot more. So I guess you could say that they're about even, mentally.

"Now, this is what I want: the complete and exclusive story of what they're working on now. It won't be easy, because they don't want to give out any information. And they're smart enough to be able to keep a secret for a long, long time. That's why I want you to take the job. I wouldn't think of giving it to anybody else on the staff."

Jocelyn smiled. "I'm smart too. Is that what you mean?"

"Sure you're smart. Maybe, even, you're smart enough to get the story.... Oh, one more thing. They're both a little childish in some ways. They have a habit of playing practical jokes on people. Don't let them joke you out of the story."

"I won't," said Jocelyn Earle. "That's all?" she asked, rising.

"That's enough, isn't it?" her employer said. "What are you going to do?"

"I don't know yet. But don't worry about it— I'll try to have the story by deadline tomorrow. Goodbye."

"Goodbye," said her employer, and Jocelyn Earle walked out of the room. . . .

"And there goes another tube, Art," called Gaynor. "Shot to hell."

Clair walked over to the meter board with a sigh, stripping off his gloves as he came. "The damn things act so funny. They test fine, no flaws, and the math says they ought to work. But you shoot the juice into them, and all that's left when the smoke clears away is a thoroughly ruptured tube. Why do you suppose that is, Paul?"

He got no answer from Gaynor but a strangling gasp. He looked up to find his colleague pointing at the door, his face a mask of horror. There stood a hideous creature, presumably female, apparently Scandinavian. "Ay bane call from de agency," it said.

Gaynor recovered himself first, and asked,

"How the hell did you get through seven locked doors, woman? What do you want?"

The creature began to talk rapidly and excitedly, and the two scientists looked at each other. "This is just like the Nobel ceremony," howled Clair over the woman's voice. "What do you suppose she's saying?"

"Haven't the faintest notion. Let's sit down. Let's kill her. Let's do something to shut her up. How about a shot of static at her?"

"Should help," agreed Clair. He swung a cumbersome machine on the figure in the door and pressed a button. A feeble but spectacular bolt of electricity shot at the woman with a roar, pinking her neatly. Suddenly her stream of Swedish was shut off. "You brace of heels!" she snapped. "If you don't know how to treat a lady, I'm leaving."

Gaynor sprang for the door and slammed it. "No," he said, "not until you explain— " But she cut him off with a snake-swift clip of the palm to his solar plexus and he folded. Clair swung a switch and the machine roared again, this time louder, and the woman fell beside Gaynor.

Clair knelt and felt his colleague's pulse. "She moves fast, that one" said Gaynor, without opening his eyes. "Did you get her?"

"Sure—with just enough static to put her out for a while. Get some cable and we'll see what kind of scrub-woman can breeze through locked doors."

They tied her securely; then Clair unceremoniously dumped a bucket of water over her. She came to with a sputter and gasp. "Was that thing a death-ray?" she asked with professional interest.

"No. Just high tension. Who are you and what's your business with us?"

"With a hefty tug you can take off my wig," the woman answered. Gaynor laid hold of a strand of hair and pulled. "My God!" he cried. "Her face comes with it!"

"Mask," she said briefly. "I am a reporter for the *Helio*, name being Earle. I want to congratulate you gentlemen. This get-up fooled Billikin, Zwei-stein, and Current. You aren't the ordinary brand of scientist."

"Nor are you the ordinary brand of reporter," said Clair raptly studying her cameo-like features. "Gaynor, you ape, untie the lady."

"Not I," said his colleague hastily backing away. "It's your turn to get socked."

"I promise to behave," she said with a smile. Reluctantly the scientist cut the cables that confined her and she rose. "Do you mind if I take off this thing?" she asked indicating her horrible dress. The men stared; Clair finally said, "Not at all."

She pulled a long slide-fastener somewhere in the garment and it fell away to reveal a modish street-outfit. Gaynor gulped strangely. "Won't you sit down, Miss Oil," he said.

She settled gracefully into a chair. "Earle," she corrected him. Clair was looking fixedly at an out-of-date periodic table tacked high on the wall, aware that this peculiar woman was studying him. Ap-provingly? he wondered.

"Now, just what was it that you wanted with us, Miss Earle," he inquired. "Maybe we can work out some arrangement...."

II. The *Prototype*

If Jocelyn hadn't been a pretty girl, the deal would never have been made. But pretty Jocelyn was, and moreover she was smart enough to capitalize on her good looks.

So, it was decided that Jocelyn, in return for a promise of strict secrecy until the experiment was concluded, would be included in the maneuvers of the two scientists, would have every opportunity of finding things out and a promise that no other paper would get a crumb of information. That was a very good bargain, for Jocelyn didn't have to put anything at all up in exchange. She was pretty, and smart. That was enough.

"Maybe I can help you two great minds anyhow," she said. "What're you trying to do?"

The two looked at each other. Finally Gaynor said: "You're not a mathematician, Miss—Jocelyn, that is. I don't know whether we can translate our language into yours. But—maybe you've heard of protomagnetism?"

"No. What is it?"

"Well, proto—we'll call it proto for short—is something like ordinary magnetism. Only this: ordinary magnetism attracts steel and iron, principally, and only to a very slight degree anything else—such as, for instance, copper and cobalt, which respond just the tiniest bit. Proto attracts a bunch of elements a little, but so little that it's never been noticed before. For instance, it attracts radium, niton, uranium, and thorium—the radioactive group—a little. The more radioactive, the greater the attraction. And the thing it attracts most of all is the new artificial Element 99.

"Another difference—magnetism, generally speaking, is a force exerted between two particles of iron or whatever. Proto, on the other hand, ain't. Radium doesn't attract radium—both particles are attracted by something else."

"Tell her which way they're attracted," interjected Clair.

"I was coming to that," started Gaynor, but Jocelyn interrupted with: "What am I supposed to gather from all this? According to my boss, you've got some sort of a ship. That's what he sent me here for: to find out what this ship was, and what you're going to do with it."

Clair was startled. "So it's an open secret now," he said to Gaynor.

"Oh, no," said Jocelyn; "but I know there's a ship. I don't know what kind of a ship it is, but I know it's there. That's all we could find out. Now, if you will kindly stop stalling and live up to your end of the bargain . . ."

"I wasn't stalling, though," said Gaynor resentfully. "That's what I was going to tell you, that we've got the *Prototype,* and we're just about ready to use it. And, what's more, you're coming along, because that's *your* part of the bargain. It wasn't before, but it is now, because I just made it so."

"Fine," said Jocelyn, unperturbed. "But where are we going?"

"That's what I was coming to— " ("It's been a long time coming," murmured Jocelyn). "We're going to the place whence comes proto. What Art was driving at a while ago is that proto doesn't pull things upward or downward, or backward or frontward or North-by-East-half-a-point-East, for that matter. It pulls them—out. Into another dimension—or so we think."

"Oh," said Jocelyn. "You mean you've got a time machine. How nice. Well thanks a lot for letting me see you fellows, and don't worry about my keeping your secret. I won't tell. And I want . . ."

"What's the matter?" asked Gaynor blankly.

Jocelyn stared at him. "You're trying to trick me, that's all. And you're not going to get away with it. Time machines are impossible. And if you think you've got one—I'm going home."

"But stop, Jocelyn," cried Gaynor. "We know time machines are impossible. We didn't say it was a time machine—you did. As a matter of fact, it probably isn't a time machine."

"As a matter of *fact,*" Clair chimed in sourly, "we don't know *what* it is."

Jocelyn looked up at that. "Sure you're not joking?" They both nodded vehemently. She hesitated, then,

"You know," she said, "I think I'm going to like this."

An hour later, Gaynor was finishing the job of explaining things to Jocelyn while Clair finished hooking up connections in the lab in the next room.

"This tube," Gaynor was saying, "is the keystone of our work. The thing inside that looks like a buckshot is composed of what will be Element 99 when the power is turned on. There's a lot of gadgets in here that you wouldn't understand if I explained them to you, but take it from me that I did a fine job in designing this tube. Consider: 99 is artificial, and it's pretty unstable. I had to incorporate the equipment for building it up and sustaining it. 99 is also radioactive, and I had to shield it to keep you, me, and the machine from crumbling into little glowing lumps. Those together ought to mean about five hundred pounds of equipment, but that was around four hundred and ninety-five more than I could get away with, because of the lack of storage space in the Prototype. So I condensed it to this." With which effusion he hefted the article in his hand. It fell to the floor with a crunch, its delicate members battered out of shape and its finely fused tubes shattered into bits.

"I see," said Jocelyn. "A neat bit of human interest. Was that the last one?"

"No," said Gaynor somberly. "We have a couple left." He took another from a locker and as they walked from the storeroom cast a glance back at the mess on the floor. "It looked a little defective anyhow," he said.

In the lab, Clair assigned the girl a place at a rheostat. "When the buzzer buzzes," he said, "open it wide and stand back." The tube was inserted, insulated, and tested, and the three took their various places, Clair gave the signal, and the circuits were closed in perfect order. They stared at the tube. It brightened, glowed, and then—smashed wide open without an apparent reason.

Clair opened the master circuit, looked up. "It did it again," he said wearily. "Why?"

"Yeah, why?" echoed Gaynor.

"Why what?" asked Jocelyn. "Why did it break, you mean?"

"Yeah," said Clair dispiritedly.

"Isn't it supposed to do that? When the proto pulls it?"

Gaynor glared at her. "Sure the proto pulls it, and— Hey! That *is* what it's supposed to do!"

Clair sat down heavily. "It sure is," he agreed. "Of all the damn fools, Paul, you and I..."

Gaynor was galvanized. "So all we have to do, Art, all we have to do is make the tube strong enough to take the ship with it when it begins pulling!"

"Did I solve something?" asked Jocelyn, a little bewildered. No one paid any attention to her. All of a sudden, they were hard at work.

III. Einstein's Extreme

Physicists generally have swarms of helpers and technicians to do all the rough, tough manual labor required in their work. This is for two reasons: because successful physicists are generally in their nineties and unable to lift anything much heavier than a gavel at an alumni meeting, and because it is considered by the majority demeaning for a mind-worker to use his hands.

That is only one of the many ways in which Gaynor and Clair differed from the Genus Physicist. They were young and strong enough to lift anything within reason and they had cranes for the stuff that was unreasonable and yet had to be lifted.

And they couldn't afford to have anyone but themselves—and Miss Earle—in their lab. If anyone knew then everyone might. An irresponsible writer or reporter would scatter the news broadcast and effectively gum up their immense undertaking.

So Gaynor, Clair, and Jocelyn did every last screw-turn and rivet-spread in the creation of the *Prototype*.

In about two weeks the job was done. Their ship was ready, a squat but very beautiful object in the eyes of its creators. The installation was complete; it was ready for the test.

Jocelyn took final notes. "Three dozen eggs," she read from a list.

"Check," said Clair, passing them to Gaynor who stacked the boxes neatly in the ship's compact refrigeration unit.

"Six pound of bacon . . ."

"And that," she said, "is the last of the food. Now, perhaps, you'll tell me why you wanted enough provisions for a month?"

Evasively, Clair answered, "You never can tell. We may like it so much out there that we'll decide to stay awhile."

Gaynor descended from the *Prototype's* main port. "Yeah," he said. "The lady's right. I am a physicist, Art, a physicist. Not a porter. And I do not enjoy carrying sacks of sugar and cans of corn. I don't know why I *should* be carrying this junk, anyway. We're not going to be gone long—presumably. If the gadgets work, two days. If not—not."

Clair chewed his thumbnail. "You never can tell," he said. "Maybe I can have a hunch myself, once in a while." He stood up and said abruptly, "Get your pencils and paper, Jocelyn. I guess we're leaving—now."

Silently, the girl gathered her notebooks up from a table and stepped into the ship. Clair swung home a last switch in the lab and passed through the bulkhead. He slammed and sealed the door. Flatly, he said, "We don't know what to expect in the line of atmosphere out there."

Gaynor took his position at the power receiver. Clair stood at the control. "I'm ready when you are, Paul," he said.

His colleague flipped a switch, a relay clicked, and the indicator arced over to the right. "Power on, Art," he said softly. And Clair closed the prime contact. Slowly the tube warmed up, glimmering with a purplish light. That was the bottle of glass and the maze of wires that was to pull them from one dimension and hurl them into another.

He slowly, s-l-o-w-l-y, pulled over a rheostat, and the tube slowly brightened.

And nothing else happened. That was all. The tube got brighter.

Desperately, angrily, Clair shoved the rheostat all the way over. And nothing, nothing at all, still seemed to have happened.

Gaynor cried sharply, "What's the matter?"

Clair said nothing. There was nothing to say. A half a year of work seemed to be wasted. And the finest chance of exploring ever given mortal men seemed to have been snatched away as a mirage. Suddenly Jocelyn screamed. "Look," she cried. "The window!" The two men turned and gasped at the sight before them.

"That isn't the lab," whispered Gaynor. "Not in a million years. We're outside, Art. *We've done it!*"

Clair stared through the quartz plate. The scene that met his eyes was incredible—un-Earthly. It was *new*, he thought. A blankness that had yet to be moulded into a thing more definite. Without shape, dimension or duration, it was—Outside.

"But what place is this, Paul? It's not space, not even space in another universe. It's no planet that could ever exist. It's not like anything that's logical at all."

"You're right. God knows. I don't think that I could give a name to this place. I don't think that any man could. Could you even hope to describe it to anyone, Jocelyn?"

"Not if I knew more words than Shakespeare. Paul—if this is nowhere near the lab or even our universe—why is gravitation in the ship normal as far as I can see?"

Gaynor smiled. "Awfully simple, woman," he said. "Obviously we have artifical gravity. We invented it almost a month ago. And—by the way—this is a spaceship too. We installed a gravity-drive.

"Now then, Art, get away from that window

and rig up the cameras. Jocelyn, take notes. I'm going to fiddle with a spectroscope."

The girl balanced a pad on her knee, dashing onto paper the random notes and observations of the two men. Minutes later, Clair was trying to develop a photographic plate and let loose some particularly blistering adjectives. "Shall I take *that* down?" she asked, raising her delicate eyebrows.

"Better not," he said. "But this—this—this *lousy* pan won't come out like it should. It doesn't look like much out there, I know, but this crazy plate won't show it anyway. Come here, Pavlik!" he called. Gaynor came from the other end of the ship.

"So Dr. Clair shouts aloud in the middle of a triple spectroanalysis," he said nastily. "So Dr. Gaynor comes running to find out what disaster has endangered our valuable lives. So the spectroanalysis is ruined from beginning to end. What's eating my esteemed colleague?"

Clair held up the plate. "I'm sorry, Pavel, " he said, "but this thing won't develop. I thought that since you are the expert of this expedition and I your fumbling but well-intentioned subordinate you might diagnose this little dab's trouble."

Gaynor took the plate. "Your labored sarcasm—" he began. Then his voice trailed off. Tensely he asked, "Is this the first that you've developed or tried to?"

"Yes," said Clair. "What's that got to do with it?"

"Plenty. Did you ever hear of Kodak mining? Probably not. It was like this. In the primitive days of excavation—say 1920—radium mines were driven hit or miss, win or lose. Then some bright chap discovered that if you leave a roll of film in certain spots the film will be ruined and thus mark the spot of a radium deposit. Art, this film is ruined, having been in the presence of richly radioactive matter. Need I say more?"

Clair smote himself on the forehead. "Radioactivity—here!" he cried. "I see it all and apologize for having been a blind imbecile in the face of the facts. Let's not talk about it just yet. Let's have dinner first. Being stuck in the middle of somewhere else puts an edge on your appetite."

"Any excuse for a meal," said Jocelyn, dumping a can of beans into a heating unit. "Just like a man. And when will I be told these dazzlingly obvious facts that you two seized on and curse yourselves for being so long about it?"

"*After* dinner, woman, you will hear all," said Gaynor firmly. They sat down in silence to eat.

The dishwashing—which consisted of dropping several cans and plates into a sealed container—was accomplished, and the three lit cigarettes. Jocelyn placed herself obtrusively before the two physicists and demanded, "Secret. Now."

Vaguely Clair began, "I don't exactly know. It's just that we have a feeling we're out of time entirely. Indications show that we've been pulled out of our own universe and not just chucked into another one at random, but that we've been slung outside of all the universes that ever were." He examined the tip of his cigarette intently, crossing his eyes.

"Damn it!" cried the girl. "And damn it twice! We have to be *somewhere*, don't we?"

"Obviously, my dear," said Gaynor soothingly. "And so we are. But as nearly as I can see, we aren't in any space-time that's ever been used before. We've got a brand new one all to ourselves. It must sound like boasting, I know, but I think we *created* this hunk of nothing."

Jocelyn began to laugh. "Well," she finally gurgled, "we sure made one lousy job of it! Listen, Messrs. Jehovah—why haven't we got a nice spot to land on? This seems to be an awfully big universe for just the *Prototype* and us three."

"Sure; it has to be," answered Clair seriously. "Einstein announced to a breathless world a long time ago: 'The more matter, the less space; the more space the less matter.' We are probably the closest approach that ever has or ever will be made to one of his limiting extremes—a universe of all space and no matter."

"Excuse me," said Jocelyn humbly. "The more I hear from you two enraptured scientists the stupider I feel. But would you mind explaining that no doubt pertinent axiom of Mr. Einstein? It seems very silly. I mean, the more space is displaced by matter, the less space there is. Obviously—no. I mean the less space—that is, matter—the less matter in a universe the more room there must be for space!"

The men looked at each other. "'Space displaced by matter.'" said Gaynor pityingly.

"'Room for space,'" Clair richly announced, rolling the phrase over his tongue.

"I'd feel a lot safer in recommending a good book on the subject, but roughly what Einstein implied was this," said Clair. "Space isn't nothing. Or, putting it differently, it *is* something. Since you don't know math, I can best describe it as a thin, weary substance partly squamous and partly rugous. Its most striking property is that when it surrounds—or penetrates—or engenders—what is called matter, which is only space, but somewhat thicker and more alert, there is a certain amount of strain.

"So naturally space gives somewhat at the seams. It wrinkles and curves all out of shape—but space, when it is curving keeps right on extending itself, and so it sort of grows crooked. In its extension it keeps on until it meets itself coming back, thereby generating a closed curve.

"Obviously the more matter the bigger a beating space takes and the sharper it curves and the sooner it meets itself. So then the closed curve is smaller and more limiting of itself."

"Thank you," said Jocelyn sweetly. "I'm sorry I asked you in the first place."

"Never mind that cad," said Gaynor indignantly. "When we get back you can tell your friends that not only did you have a whole universe practically to yourself but that yours was at least three billion times bigger than theirs."

"Speaking of getting back," Clair interrupted. "What shall we do now? There isn't anything to see here—want to get home? Or shall we wait here and dope out some way of getting somewhere else where there is something to see?"

"We can't do that, Art. At least I don't want to try. If we start breaking into brand-new frames we may get so lost that we won't even remember we have a home. We'd better just scat. As it is I'm licking my lips over what we're going to tell the honorable academy of science. Hell, we've seen enough here to leave us limp—even though all we've seen is nothing."

Clair nodded, but a bit wistfully. There were lots of things that could be done here—lots of places to be visited from this jumping-off point.

"We're on our way, then," he said. "Position, Paul. Let's tap the broadcast." Jocelyn looked a question, so he explained. "We're using our own system of beam-power. Naturally, we couldn't carry enough."

Gaynor turned the switch on the audio receiver. A second passed as the tubes warmed up; then a faint hum.

"God, Art, but that's dim," he said worriedly.

Clair was equally perturbed. "Yeah—try to tap it now. There's no use stalling. Even if we don't get enough power to just slap us back we might accumulate enough to limp home."

Gaynor shrugged his shoulders and closed another switch. The dial quivered and swung over. Then seconds crawled by, and then the automatic relays in the lab seemed to have reacted, because the power intake needle quivered faintly. It came to rest at a point infinitesimally removed from zero. "Faint is right," said Gaynor.

Clair touched the prime switch. Nothing happened. The tube didn't even glow.

He shoved the rheostat over viciously. At the very peak-end of its arc, when the power flowing through the tube under normal conditions would have been inconceivable, the tractor tube very faintly reddened.

And that was all. With common accord the three voyagers looked out of the window. The scene had not changed an iota. Blackness swirled indescribably before them, on the other side of a meager inch of metal, quartz, and plastic.

IV. Baby Universe

A full minute passed as they stared out of the port. Jocelyn interrupted the dismal silence with, "It looks as if we'll have to plan on being here for a hell of a long time, gentlemen. Apparently, I'll never write those feature stories."

"Yeah," said Clair vaguely. "A hell of a long time." He cut off the trickle of power, and the indicator needle ticked back to zero. "Maybe we'd better get some sleep," he said. "We might dream of a solution."

Silently Gaynor swung down the three bunks and drew curtains between them, and they vanished into their improvised compartments.

Clair was nearly asleep when Gaynor hissed at him through the thin barrier. "What do you want now?" he asked drearily.

"It occurs to me," said Gaynor, "that we've made a mistake."

"That's about as obvious an understatement as ever I've heard in a long and aimless career. What do you mean?"

"Listen: the logical train is as follows. We haven't figured a way out because we have no power. And if we have no power we have no proto. And if we have no proto we have no pull. And now, colleague, tell me just what good it would do us if we had any power?"

"Pavlik, I'm too tired for riddles. What have you found?"

"Just this—proto *attracts* 99. It doesn't re*pel* it. It can't attract us any closer because we're where the proto comes from in the first place. So even if we build up the 99—what happens then? There wouldn't be any effect!"

"Then that means," said Clair, suddenly tense, "we've reached a perfect impasse. You're right, of course. But it doesn't do us any good. Less than no good at all, in fact, because now we know that we wouldn't know how to get away if we had the power in the first place."

"Then that sums it up," said Gaynor bitterly. "We not only can't get out, but we don't know how we could get out if we could. Funny things happen to logic when you have a universe all to yourself."

Suddenly Jocelyn's sleepy voice rang out. "What," it said, "are you two conspirators muttering about? Are you planning to sacrifice the sacred virgin to the Great God Proto?"

"We've just decided," said Gaynor dolefully, "that we're here almost for good. Or at least that we'll be here until the vapor pressure of our bodies disperses us uniformly through our universe—which, as any chemist will tell you, is a long and longer time."

"Good," she said astonishingly. "Now that you've decided maybe you can get some sleep. Good night, all."

"A very unusual girl," whispered Clair hoarsely. "If it didn't seem sort of silly under the circumstances I'd propose to her."

"And what makes you think," snapped Gaynor nastily, "that she'd have you? In fact, I had some thoughts along that line myself. Do you mind, esteemed colleague?"

"Not at all. Maybe it'll come down to the flip of a coin."

There was a long pause. Then Gaynor said nervously, "Do you suppose, Art, that we'll have to eat one another?"

"What's that?"

"You know. Cannibalism. It's customary."

"No," said Clair thoughtfully. "It would be irrational in this case. Cannibalism is called for only when there is a question of outside influence. Thus, if we were waiting to be saved by a passing space-scow there would be some point to it; that is, one might survive and live a full life at the expense of the others. However in our case while we might eat Miss Earle on running out of food the chance of survival is too small to counterbalance the degradation of human instincts involved.

"I took the precaution of hiding a bottle of Scotch—where *you'll* never find it, esteemed colleague—and we have enough medicine aboard to furnish us with an overdose of any variety we desire. So we simply dump some veronal into goblets, add a few jiggers, touch glasses, and say goodbye."

"Thanks, Art," said Gaynor gratefully. "You think of everything. Well—good night."

"Good night."

Breakfast was a grim and desultory affair. To raise their spirits they were playing a sort of word game. It circled gruesomely about the adjective, "apodyctic." Jocelyn would ask, "Am I apodyctic?" and the two men would airily answer that she was and so were they and the ship and breakfast and plumbers' pipe and suspenders. "But," said Gaynor ominously, "a Springfield rifle is *not*."

"Well, then—is the window apodyctic?"

The two physicists looked at each other. "I'm inclined to think that it is," said Gaynor reflectively.

"I don't know," mused Clair, glancing at the little square of quartz. Then—

"My God!" he cried thinly. "Look at that!"

The others spun around and stared. The amorphous, stirless utter black that had been outside the port was there no longer. Instead there was motion and a mad spectrograph of colors which blended into a sort of gray sworl. A congeries of glowing spheres blazed past the window. Great looping ribbons of flame snaked past them and curled around the ship cracking quietly to themselves as they struck.

The darkness was light, and the silence was sound; they stared and saw depth of space beyond vast depth; incredible shapes and sizes and colors stirring and awakening for as far as the eye could see. Vague, glowing areas weirdly collapsed into tense spheres that screamed off in any direction. Vast shapes smashed into each other to explode into far-scattering pellets of blazing green or blue or gold.

Huge gouts of flame assailed one another. An incredibly vast rod of light that must have rivalled a solar system for magnitude collided with a great, spinning disk and absorbed it, then swelled and shattered into a million fragments that blazed with all the lights of the stars and shot off in unison to some distant goal.

Globes battled with one another near the ship, lancing out immense spears of gleaming force, smashing at each other in Jovian combat, ravening their might into the incredible void. A nebulous anthropomorphic figure the size of a galaxy strode immensely through the deeps to crumble into vast glowing discs as it neared a mighty ophidian of flame.

The three voyagers stared insanely at the colossal spectacle, nearer to madness than a human being can safely approach. It was Jocelyn who slammed the metal shutter against the port, shutting out the awful view.

"Sit down," she commanded. "You've seen all you can stand of *that*." Limply the two men obeyed.

"I don't think dying would matter much to me now, Art," said Gaynor flatly. "What was happening out there?"

Stupidly, pedantically, Clair said, "Every accepted cosmogony states that at one time the entire universe consisted of a single homogeneous spread of matter-energy permeating all of space. They say that this all-embracing and infinitely tenuous cloud was at absolute rest with neither motion nor the possibility of motion. There was not, there could not have been thesis or antithesis or synthesis.

"Nobody knows what happened to it after that, before it became what it is today, with most of it vacuum and the rest of it densely packed matter and energy."

"I see," said Gaynor. "What's going on—outside—is the birth of a universe. Or perhaps only its birth-pains. As yet there is no law save that law must struggle to assert itself over the insanity of matter and energy on the loose. Possibly this primitive stress-material has a will of its own—at least that's one explanation of what we saw. Possibly the eternal combat-motif is merely the expression of the ascendancy of law so long outraged by the impossible state of rest that obtained for so long...

"At any rate we have to thank the stress-material for holding out so valiantly against law—otherwise we'd not be here."

"What do you mean by that?" snapped Clair.

"Just this. That the stress-material is *grateful*. You see, we have created this universe and *waked it into life*. It is this ship that monkey-wrenched the quiescent machinery of the dead cosmos into existence. *What is outside we have done*.

"We are in the storm-center of the storm we have created; if law had its way we would have been the first item to be destroyed by these incredible forces. However, though it may sound insane, the stress-material displays a touching filial affection toward its parent and so forbears.

"Possibly that is madness. I don't know how long we have before the junk outside knuckles under to dialectics and so destroys us. It may be twenty seconds and it may be twenty billion years."

Clair stared at him, fascinated. "You get the damnedest notions, Paul," he breathed. "But you *must* be right. Take notes, Jocelyn.

"Memorandum to the academy of science—it has been definitely established that the uniform stress state will obtain until a foreign body provides the center of gravity which, in an infinity or closed-circle finity, which amounts to the same thing, is lacking. The uniform stress state does not appear to be a product of mutual attraction, for attraction in any direction is counterbalanced by an exactly equal attraction to the particles in any other direction."

"Shall I mail this right away," asked Jocelyn sourly, "or do you want to see the transcript?"

Clair smote his forehead. "Very true," he said. "But I wish I could see Billikin's face when and if he hears of this!" His face changed suddenly. "I'll bet," he said, "he hears of this whether he knows it or not!"

"What does that mean?" asked Gaynor.

"Pavlik, you thick-skulled ape! Did you ever bother to think of *what* universe we're so busy creating? *Our own!*

"Don't you see? We *couldn't* have just stepped outside of space and stayed there for any length of time. We must have been snatched out for just as long as we had the power on, and as soon as it was cut off we slipped back into our own universe—the easy way! That is, the easiest point of entry is at either the beginning or the end, and we happened on the beginning.

"This little chunk of matter—the *Prototype*—slipped down the entropy gradient, slipped right up again, and busted the mechanics of a static system wide open!"

"So," said Gaynor, "this is the beginning and not the end."

"Sure!" cried Clair.

"How do you tell one from another, esteemed collaborator?"

Clair's face fell. "All right," he said—"what if it is the end instead? We've started it going all over again, so what's the difference?"

"None," said Gaynor.

"Excuse me, gentlemen," Jocelyn interrupted demurely. "To my girlish mind you have strayed far from the essential point. That is—getting the hell out of here. The problem is no less acute despite our newly-discovered godlike qualities. There appears to be an entirely new set of data to work on, and I humbly submit that you get to work on them with an eye to slapping us back into something vaguely resembling a happy home."

"My old grandmother told me once," said Gaynor thoughtfully, "'If you can't drink on a problem, sleep on it. And if you can't sleep on it, eat on it.' She was a crazy old girl. Let's have some lunch, I suggest soup topped with whipped cream, omelette surrounding a heaping platter of fried canned chicken, to be wound up with stewed pineapple and brandied cherries."

"Much as it pains me to contradict you," said Jocelyn firmly, "we're having beans. Hundreds and hundreds of them—not only nourishing but tasty. Not only tasty but economical. Besides, we have to watch our provisions and figures."

They also had to watch their stock of tobacco. In fact they split a cigarette three ways after eating and nearly set fire to Clair's soup-strainer lighting the segments.

"Now," said Gaynor, puffing gingerly, "we know we're not where we thought we were. The question before the house is, how do we get where we want to be?"

"We know," said Jocelyn, "that the utterly useless trickle of juice from the lab is now effectively gimmicked by all the static zipping around outside. We have a generator here which is too incredibly feeble for our purposes to be anything but a lawn ornament. The crying need is power."

Clair mused, "It would be nice if we were outside this infant universe, or at least in a middle-aged one."

"Hold it, Art," snapped Gaynor. "You said outside? Maybe there's all the power we need out there beyond the hull!"

"Yeah—but it'll be a million million years before it's in any form that we can use." He snuffed out his stub of cigarette. "Or maybe—what the hell! If we do get power enough how're we going to make proto out of it?"

"Remember that photo plate, Art?" asked Gaynor.

"Yeah. Radioactive." Then he snapped erect and shouted it, *"Radioactive!* Everything in this whole damned universe—we're saved, it seems, Paul. You're right—we don't have to build up 99— *we've got it right outside!"*

V. Pixies

It had taken them a week and a day to lead-sheath a reservoir for the radioactive gasses and to build and sheath a suction pump capable of drawing them in.

"Stand by," said Clair shortly. "Power on."

Gaynor threw the switch of their small, compact generator and Clair focused the electric lens with difficulty on the bulk of the gasses. "Ten seconds," Jocelyn finally announced. "Power off." They had felt nothing. Clair nervously strode to the window. They kept it covered, now. Hesitating a moment he flung the shutter open. The scene had not changed— they were still stranded. "Well, Paul," he asked simply. "Now what—we haven't moved."

"No?" asked Jocelyn sweetly. "Then what do you call *that?"*

They followed her gaze out of the port. She had, it seemed, been referring to a squadron of flying dragons that were winging their way towards the ship in a perfect V-formation.

"That," said Clair flinging the drivers into 'full speed ahead,' "I call a mistake."

Gaynor moaned gently. "That's no stress-energy. Used to have dreams like this," he gibbered. "Only they weren't quite so big and they didn't breath quite so much flame and they always turned into snakes before they curled up on my chest."

"Planet ahead," said Jocelyn. "It's all alone—hasn't got a sun. What do you make of it?"

"I'm sure I don't know," said Clair wearily. "But I'm going to land there. Being chased by flying dragons—especially flying dragons that can fly in a vacuum—is getting us nowhere."

"It's getting us onto that planet," said Jocelyn, "and I don't like its looks."

"We'll land and see what happens first," said Clair, the dominant male. They were hanging over the surface of the globe about a mile up. Suddenly it gulped at them. A huge mouth, the size of one of the Great Lakes, opened in its surface and gulped at them. "Will we?" asked Jocelyn.

"No," said Clair unhappily. "I suppose not." The ship drove on.

Jocelyn laughed madly. "Pixies off the starboard bow," she said in a flat, hysterical voice.

"Yeah?" said Gaynor skeptically. Then he looked. His eyes bulged and his mouth opened and closed apoplectically. "Where the hell are we!" he screamed. "Fairy-land?"

For pixies they were—a gauzy, fluttering band of them!

"Maybe," said Gaynor, "they'll chase off the dragons." But they made no move to do so. Instead they were keeping pace with the ship and rigging up a nasty-looking device with handles and snouts.

"I think," said Jocelyn, "that the Little People plan to do us dirt."

And sundry polychromatic rays shot from the device and struck the ship.

"That tears it!" screamed Gaynor. He flung the dynamo into operation and snapped the lens into focus. Abruptly, they found themselves back in the nascent universe they knew so well, pyrotechnics and all. Jocelyn closed the shutter.

"Now," she said, "teacher offers a big prize to the bright little boy who can tell her what that ghastly district was and why we got there."

Clair and Gaynor stared at her from the floor. "I'm sure I don't know," said Clair dully. "Whatever it was it was awfully silly."

Gaynor moaned, "Flying dragons! I thought I'd left them behind when I had my twenty-first birthday. And dammit, I'm sore at those pixies. They were untraditional. If they'd been imps with spiked tails it would have been understandable—they're expected to muck things up in general. Now, Clair— where were we, the lady asked. I'll consult our instruments."

He rose painfully and opened a graph-box to refer to the continuous record of flight maintained by the tracing needles on endless scrolls of paper.

"I think," he said, "that I know what happened.

"We must hold in mind the unassailable fact that all atoms are similarly constituted in form and all similarly constituted as regards their dynamics. That is to say, the electrons move all in a certain direction at a certain rate of speed.

"This is true of planets and the atoms that compose them; of the atoms that compose our bodies and our sensory organs in particular.

"*Now*—obviously these sensory organs will perceive only that type of atom which is similar to it in its major characteristics. For example, the eye will not take heed of a substance whose atoms are spinning backwards in relation to the atoms of the eye. But if the atoms of the eye are reversed in their motion they will readily perceive the matter whose electrons are now moving in a similar direction."

Clair said succinctly, "So what?"

"That, esteemed colleague, is what happened to us and the ship. That nasty place we came from is *backwards*—in the larger sense, I mean."

Jocelyn looked baffled. "Then I was turned upside-down and inside-out to see those nasty people? All I can say is that it was hardly worth the trouble!"

"But," puzzled Gaynor, "why should those creatures be the dead spit and image of all our mythological and childhood bogies?"

"I'm sure I wouldn't know. Quite probably, though, those things can slink through, or at least did slink through at one time to scare the hell out of our ancestors back in the ages primitive. Or possibly our inspired spinners of folklore had something a little wrong with their eyes. It may be that a rod or cone in the retina is peculiar and lets through misty shapes that belong actually to the reverse universe."

"You're probably right," said Jocelyn unexpectedly. "And little children that swear they see fairies and goblins—they must belong in the same class. Sometimes funny things can leak through. We're being frightful iconoclasts this trip—repudiating gravity, cosmogony, and etherics in one breath and establishing folklore in the next as scientific fact."

"Very true," said Clair. "But this cuts no ice. We made a mistake that time somewhere—will it happen again, Pavlik?"

"I don't see why it should," said Gaynor. "Maybe it works alternately. We can try it."

Automatically, he took his place at the power-intake equipment with one hand on the switch that controlled the generator.

"Hold on," said Jocelyn. "If we're getting out of this mess I don't see why we shouldn't celebrate."

The two men looked at one another. "Incredible girl," said Gaynor. Clair said nothing, but reached into the core of an electromagnet and drew out a gleaming three-liter tube bearing the nobel imprint of the House of MacTeague.

"Voici le Scotch," he pronounced with pride. "Get paper cups, Pavlik."

They poured shots of the liquor and touched glasses.

"To the voyage," said Jocelyn.

"To Jocelyn," announced the men in chorus.

They tossed their cups into a refuse container and took their stations. Clair juggled the lens about, adjusting it precisely.

"Power on," he said quietly.

Gaynor threw the switch of the generator, and the power trickled through—perhaps forty thousand volts. There was a dull roaring through the apparatus as Clair swung in the prime switch and moved over the rheostat. Suddenly he was afraid—what if they had been wrong? What if they hadn't moved, and were locked forever within a limitless prison of space? "Ten seconds," he said licking his lips.

Jocelyn opened the shutter with a gesture that had in it something of defiance. There, twinkling before them were a myriad points of light that cut into their souls like icy knives.

Quietly she said, "'Thence issuing, we again beheld the stars.'"

VI. Stars and Men

The universe they were in was an agreeably middle-aged one, with few giants and a majority of dwarf suns. They didn't know whether it was theirs or one similar, and they didn't much care. They knew that they had only to encounter a reasonably civilized race to provide them with equipment and perhaps some days that were not endless struggle to survive.

What the three voyagers needed was rest. Their chronometer lopped the day into three arbitrary sections which saw always one asleep, one at the lookout plate and one handling the powerful driving engines. They roared along at a speed inconceivable, yet traveling two weeks before the nearest star became apparent as a disk.

Jocelyn was at the port sighting the body with an instrument that would give them its approximate distance, size, and character. "About five hours away from a landing," she announced. "Type, red giant."

"Five hours?" asked Gaynor.

"Right. I can't see planets yet, if there are any. I don't know that they're typical of giant stars."

"There may be some," said Gaynor, his fingers feeling the pulse of fluid in a tube. "And they may be inhabited. And the people may be advanced enough to give us what we want. Then it's home for us all—eh? Maybe you'll get your articles printed after all."

Her haggard face curved into a smile. "And maybe you'll see the look on Billikin's face when you show him those formulae."

"Maybe. Somehow I don't feel inclined to doubt it."

Their chronometer uttered a sharp warning peal, and Clair was awake at once. "To bed, woman," he said. "The dominant male takes over." She handed him the instrument and the slip of paper on which her calculations had been made, and with a feeble gesture of hope and cheer for both of them disappeared behind her curtain.

"Extraordinary woman," said Clair after a pause.

"Yeah. I don't see how she keeps going."

"I'm damned if I see how any of us keep going!" cried Clair with a sudden burst of temper.

Gaynor looked at him sharply. "Hold on to yourself, Art," he said. "As the lion said, it always gets darker before it gets lighter. How about that sun out there? Take an observation, will you?"

Clair adjusted the minute lenses and mirrors of the device and read off the result from its calibrated scale. "About three hours at our present rate. But its gravity'll take hold and speed us up most helpful. I think I see a planet."

"Look again—I think you're mistaken."

"Right—I am. It's a meteorite headed our way. Deflect to the left a few degrees if you want to stay healthy."

The ship veered sharply and a great, dark body passed them in silence.

"Maybe we'd better dodge that sun entirely, Paul," said Clair. "It might drag us in."

"I have my reasons for taking this course. Look at the fuel tank," said Gaynor shortly.

Clair bent over the panel of dials that was the heart of the ship. He read aloud from an indicator. "Twenty-three liters of driving juice left." There was a long pause. "Pretty bad, isn't it, Paul?"

"Extremely so. When we get near enough that sun I'm going to play its gravity for all its worth. We have to get somewhere fast or we don't get anywhere at all. . . .

"By the way," he added, "Jocelyn doesn't know where we stand with the fuel. Suppose we don't let her know until she has to. Right?"

"Check," said Clair. "Maybe she has a right to know, but personally I feel more comfortable in my superior misery." He swallowed a food tablet. They were just starting on them—all the roughage diet had been consumed.

They were nearing the huge red sun, now. "Steady on the course, if you're going to take her through," said Clair. "If not, deflect up about twenty degrees and level out on three degrees of elevation."

"I'm taking her through, all right," said Gaynor grimly. "And us with her!" Reckless of the engines he clamped down an iron hand on the controls and the blunt little vessel shot forward, it speed redoubled.

The glare from the nearby sun lit up the engineroom with a feverish glow; Clair by the port seemed to be watching an Earthly sunset, the gaunt lines of his face picked out sharply by the somber light. The light grew as they swung across the face of the star, and became intolerably bright. Clair abruptly slammed the shutter of the port. "We can't risk blindness just here and now," he said thinly.

They felt the ship leap ahead under their feet; gravity was asserting itself once more as they came into the sway of the monster sun. The eyes of the two men were glued to the speed indicator. It mounted from its already incredible figure, then, as Gaynor abruptly cut off the flow of driving power, quivered down—halted—again began to mount. It rose and doubled, and the heat rose with it, beating through the thin metal walls of the vessel. Glaring streaks of light streamed through microscopic cracks in the metal shutter against the port. An indicator needle swung crazily on the instrument panel; the air and body of the ship was taking on a dangerously high potential of electricity.

Clair opened the shutter and winced as the stream of radiation hit his face. "We're past it," he said. "How's our speed?"

Gaynor examined the panel. "Constant," he said. "As soon as it lets down we can boost it with a bit of driving." He examined the potential indicator. "Look at that, Art!" he exclaimed. "God help the first meteorite that tries to get near us!"

Jocelyn appeared from behind her curtain. "Congratulations," she said. "That was a neat piece of corner-cutting. Where do we go from here?"

"I'm sure I don't know," said Gaynor wearily as the eight hour bell clanged. "Take over, Miss E." He walked to his bunk, already half asleep.

The girl swallowed a few food tablets and took the controls. "Human interest," she said.

"Sure," said Clair absently. "Great guy, Pavel."

"And what did I hear about the fuel?" she asked suddenly vicious.

"Just that there isn't enough of it," said Clair innocently. "We were worried about you worrying about it."

"I see," said the girl. "Big brother stuff. Don't let that foolish woman know. She'd only make a fuss about it when there's nothing we can do to help it. The female's place is on the farm with the other domesticated stock, huh?" She stuck her chin out belligerently.

"Excuse us," said Clair. "We were misguided

by each other. Now that you know, so what? That makes the three of us a happy little family in a happy little hearse squibbing ourselves God knows where until our fuel runs dry. Then we drift. And drift and drift and drift. So what? For a good night's sleep without that goddamn bell I'd cut your throat, young lady, and throw you to the wolves."

She laughed happily. "Now *that's* the kind of talk I like to hear." she said. "Good, honest whimsy." Then Clair laughed and started her laughing again. They were sobered somewhat by a great gout of light and a crackling roar that shook the ship from stem to stern.

"What was that?" she asked. "Or is it another one of your secrets?"

"I think we can let you in on it," he said. "Just an inoffensive meteorite that came too near us and got blown to hell for its pains. We picked up a lot of excess juice around that red giant, and we just got our chance to fire it off at something."

"Poor little meteorite!" she gurgled, and they were laughing again.

Two weeks later no laughter could be heard on the little vessel. Three haggard and gaunt human beings sprawled grotesquely on the floor. The taste of food had not been in their mouths for days, and for them there was no sleep. The stars that had been once a hope and a prayer to them glittered mockingly through their port, oblivious to so small a thing as human want.

Gaynor stirred himself. "Art," he said.

"Yeah?"

"I suppose you recall our little discussion on the ethics of cannibalism back there—Outside?"

"I hope you're not making a concrete proposal, chum. I'd hate to think so."

"No, Art. But you remember what our talk led to? Think hard, you fuzz-brained chimpanzee."

"Insults will get you nowhere at this point," interrupted Jocelyn. "What are the male animals discussing?"

"Ways and means," said Gaynor. "I'll put it this way. If you didn't want to either eat your best friends or be eaten by them and you know that unless you ceased to exist shortly you would be compelled to eat them or be eaten by them—well, what would you do?"

"I think I understand," said Jocelyn slowly. "I've read about it time and again and shuddered at the thought—but now it's different. I'd hate to eat you, little Pavlik, but if we don't—do something— we'll be thinking about it in silence and then comes the drawing of straws or the flip of a coin and one of us gets brained from behind."

"I'll get the stuff," said Clair wearily dragging himself to his feet. He was heard to smash bottles in the storeroom, then returned with the flask of whiskey and a little paper box.

The others took cups and presented them; shakily he poured the liquor, slopping on the floor as much as went into the cups.

"What does the trick?" asked Gaynor curiously.

"Mercury compound," he answered shortly, and tried to open the box. He spilled the tablets on the floor, and they bent agedly to pick theirs up.

"Two apiece is enough," said Clair thinly. They dropped the pellets into the liquid. Gaynor was delighted to see that it bubbled brightly. He inhaled the bouquet of the whiskey.

"No doubt about it in the mind of any gentlemen worth the name," he said. "House of MacTeague is far and away the best that money can buy."

"You're right, Pavlik," said Jocelyn. She rested her cup momentarily on the indicator panel. She felt as though the floor were swaying beneath her feet. "Is the ship moving?" she asked.

"No," said Gaynor. "At least, no acceleration."

Jocelyn proposed the toast: "To—us. The hunters and the hunted; the seekers and the sought; the quick and the dead. To us!"

The others didn't repeat the toast. Something was wrong. Clair spun around, his face picked out in a green glow that had never been seen before. They dropped their cups and crowded at the port. The ship was surrounded by a bright green glow that leaked even through the pores of the ship's metal hull. Gaynor turned to the speed indicator. "Look!" he cried hoarsely.

The device had smashed itself attempting to record a fabulous figure.

Back at the port they saw one star that grew.

"We're held and drawn by a beam of some sort," excitedly Clair explained. "We're headed for that sun!"

As the disk of that star grew great in their heaven the ship slowed its mad flight. They could see a planetary system now. The beam had shot from one of those worlds.

Swift as thought their vessel shot down on one of the worlds. The green beam was more intense now; they could see that it emanated from a great structure on the planet. There were lights—dams—cities—great scored lines in the surface of the world that might have been roads.

The beam suddenly became a brake; they descended slowly and in state. A great concrete plain came in view—it was the roof of a building. There were first specks, then figures standing there. As the ship came to rest through the port they could see them as people—human beings—beautiful and stately.

It wasn't Earth, nor even much like it. But it was all that they wanted it to be—a point from which they might continue their wanderings, get rest and food, equipment and knowledge to set them on the right trail for home.

NOVA MIDPLANE

I. The Gaylens

Except for Gaynor's snores, and the rustle of Clair
twitching around in the bed, the room was very quiet.
It was warm, and dusky, and altogether a pleasant
room to sleep in. . . .

Until, coming through the glass walls, light began streaming in, from a rapidly rising sun. Quickly
the room got brighter and brighter: then, suddenly,
there was a faint click from Gaynor's bed, a buzz,
and violently the bed turned over catapulting Gaynor
to the floor, where he landed with an awakening yell
and a thud. A second later, Clair's bed ejected its
occupant as well.

Clair groaned and shoved himself to his feet.
"I must be getting used to this, Paul," he said. "It
didn't bother me much today."

"You may be getting used to it. There are some
things that I'll never get used to," murmured Gaynor
drowsily, holding his head in his arms. "The gas they
use to put us to sleep every night, for instance. It
makes me itch like the devil."

"Me too," said Clair, busily inspecting his teeth

in a mirror. "I must be allergic to the stuff to some extent. We'll have to tell Gooper. Otherwise I might begin to break out with big rashes."

"And you wouldn't like that to happen to your screen-idol pan, would you?" sneered Gaynor viciously.

"Why not, bud?" snapped Clair, putting on a pair of socks weft of every color of the rainbow.

"Jocelyn might not like it—that's why not," said his friend, peering at Clair's socks, and then selecting a somewhat gaudier pair for himself.

"And what if it isn't Jocelyn?"

With a start Gaynor straightened up and stared at his companion. "If it isn't Jocelyn," he said wonderingly, "who—or what—is it?"

"My business alone."

They weren't about to slug each other as a casual observer might have supposed. Fighting words before breakfast were only one of the inexplicable habits that had kept these two together for most of their young lives.

They made a strange pair—physicists both, and in perfect symbiosis. One was a practical engineer, fully qualified to toss around murderous voltages or pack them in little glass tubes of the other's design and inspiration. Perhaps they were drawn together by a mutual love for practical jokes of the lowest sort—like rigging up chairs with high-voltage, low-wattage electrical contacts, or cooking up delicious formal dinners which crumbled into gray powder before the eyes of the horrified guest.

Be that as it may—they were here. Where here was they did not know, nor could they have any way of knowing, so, as was their way, they made the best of whatever happened to them, though their present weird fix was probably the most unexpected incident in two unpredictable careers that moved as one.

"Art," said Gaynor warningly, "Jocelyn wouldn't like for us to be late."

"Good lord!" cried Clair resonantly. "Is she waiting for us?"

"Sure she is. We were supposed to have breakfast with her. Don't you remember?"

"I thought this was screen-test day," said Clair hopelessly. "These Gaylens have the most confused notion of the number of appointments a man can keep at one time."

"We have the screen-tests after breakfast," said Gaynor. "Or that seemed to be the idea." He draped an exceptionally fancy shawl about his shoulders.

"Like it?" he said, capering before his friend.

"All right for here," said Clair grudgingly. "But don't try to get away with that on Broadway. You'd be picked up in a second."

"This isn't Broadway. Come on."

Arm in arm, they strolled down a short stretch of corridor and stepped onto an undulating platform. Gaynor kicked at a protruding stud at his feet, and the thing went into motion, carrying them to the very door of a vaulted concourse of glass. There they dismounted and looked around the immense place.

A tall girl with the pale face of a perfect cameo, save that her eyes and the corners of her mouth were touched with something that the Italian carvers of the middle ages had never dreamed could be in the face of a woman—vivacity and wit—approached them.

"Ah, friends," she said bitterly.

"Sorry we're late," said Gaynor with a soft, foolish look on his face.

"Where do we eat, Jocelyn?" asked Clair practically.

"Right over here," she said as she piloted them to a long table with curiously slung hammocks for seats. "I've ordered."

"I don't see how you pick these things up," sighed Gaynor unhappily. "I've been trying to master their menus for weeks, and still every time I want food I get glue or a keg of nails."

"They must think you're mechanically inclined. Here are the eats." Jocelyn spoke as she saw a little disk set into the table begin slowly to revolve, a signal to take off elbows and hands under pain of being scalded. The top of the table neatly flipped over, and there before them was a breakfast according to the best Gaylen tradition.

Gaynor swore under his breath as he stared with a pale face at the wormy mass before him.

"Highly nutritious, I'm told," commented Jocelyn, plunging into her dish of the same with a utensil that looked like the spawn of a gyroscope and one of the more elaborate surgical instruments.

Gaynor dug in determinedly, thinking of bacon and eggs and toast and orange juice and strong coffee—in fact, of every delicious breakfast he had ever eaten on Earth before setting off on this screwiest of all journeys ever undertaken by man.

He was staring at the empty plate with a sort of morbid fascination when a Gaylen came up to their table.

"Quite finished?" asked the Gaylen.

"Quite," said Gaynor and Clair simultaneously. "Oh, quite."

"Then we shall now go to the recording studio," said the Gaylen. "Our duty to posterity must not be delayed."

"Okay, Gooper," said Clair. "But who does the talking?"

"All of you. Or whomever you want."

They mounted the moving ramp again, this time riding far into the recesses of the building before getting off into a glass-walled room obviously very thoroughly insulated against sound and vibration.

"Address that wall," said Gooper, pointing to a black, plastered partition. He was outside the glass.

"When does it go on?" asked Jocelyn.

"It went on the moment you entered," said the Gaylen with a smile. "Now begin at the beginning."

Clair took a deep breath. Since neither of the others seemed anxious to speak, he began. "Well, my partners and I," he said, "are from a planet known as Earth—the third major satellite of a yellow dwarf star which may or may not be in this present universe. We don't know where it is—or where we are."

He stopped, waiting for one of the others to take up the tale.

"Go ahead, Art," said Gaynor. "You're doing fine."

Reluctantly, Clair continued. "Uh—well, we freely acknowledge that we never expected to get here. In fact, we weren't exactly sure that we'd ever get anywhere alive, since we were the first to experiment with a hitherto unknown—or unutilized, at least—force which we called protomagnetism.

"This force, protomagnetism, had quite a resemblance to the common phenomenon of ferromagnetism. The big difference was that it didn't act on the same substances, and that the force appeared to come from somewhere pretty strange. Where that somewhere was, we didn't know—don't know yet.

"But we built a ship—we called it the *Prototype*—which had, as its motive power, a piece of the element most favored by protomagnetism. We figured that, soon as we let it, the proto would drag on the element and pull it, together with the attached ship, to whatever place in space it came from. We also have artificial gravity for directing the ship in normal space, and plenty of food and oxygen regenerators— everything we could think of.

"That's the way we'd planned it, and that's the way it worked. I forgot to mention, though, that at the last moment we found we had to ship an extra passenger, a Miss Jocelyn Earle—the female among us—who was a newspaperwoman of sorts.

"Well—we got to the source of proto and found ourselves in a universe of perfect balance—a one hundred percent equipoise of particles distributed evenly through infinite space, each acting equally on every other. But, naturally, we upset all that. Our ship coming into that closed system was plenty sufficient to joggle a few of the particles out of position. Those particles joggled more, and more, and then the whole thing seemed to blow up in our face.

"Anyway, after a couple of false starts into some pretty weird planes and dimensions, we managed to get into this present space-time frame. This wasn't too good either, because we couldn't seem to find a planet by the hit-or-miss method. Planets were too scarce, especially the oxygen-bearing atmosphere-cum-oxidized-hydrogen hydrosphere type—unfortunately, the only type that could do us any good.

"Well—we couldn't find a planet—and we *didn't* find a planet. This planet reached out and found us. The first thing we knew, there was a tractor beam of sorts on us and we were snatched down out of the sky onto your very lovely world. Then you Gaylens crept up on us and slapped mechanical educators on us and taught us your language at the cost of a couple of bad headaches.

"It was a sort of a fantastic coincidence, we thought; until we found out that Gooper over there had been scanning the heavens for quite a while, looking for a new planet, or a wandering star, or anything that might be important enough to win him recognition. We would be ungrateful to say anything against our savior, but I admit we had some rather generally bitter reactions when we found that practically Gooper's sole reason for dragging us down out of the sky—his sole reason for having been looking at the sky, that is—was the hope of earning himself a name. One of the principal things I would like to do here is to establish our terrestrial system of nomenclature. Your way of giving every babe a serial number for identification, and making each person *earn* a name by doing something or discovering something of importance to the world may be right enough on a merit basis, but it seems to lead to complications.

"So Gooper—the one who found us—is now known as Gaynor-Clair. To avoid confusion he is known among us as Gooper."

II. Jocelyn Plays with Fire

"Thank you," said Gooper. "It's turned off now. You have made a valuable contribution to our knowledge, friends. But may I impose on your generosity with your time a little further?"

"Might as well," said Clair bitterly.

"A committee of our scientists wish to examine your ship, the *Prototype*. Will you explain to them its various functions?"

"Sure," said Gaynor. "Let's go."

They mounted the ramp and traveled a short distance.

Waiting for them was a group of about eight of their hosts, and Gooper introduced them hastily. Practically all of them had names—an accurate index of the scientific prowess of the group. One, a short, sweet-faced female, had been honored with the name of Ionic Intersection for an outstanding discovery she had made in that field. As Gooper presented her to Clair they both smiled.

"We've met already," said Clair.

"To put it mildly," laughed the girl. The Earthman shot her a warning look and muttered a word which Gaynor couldn't quite hear—though he tried. So Gaynor began the lecture by conducting his hosts through the ship.

"It's a bit crowded here," he said, "but, after all, we hadn't planned that it should be big enough to hold more than two. Most of these gadgets—air regenerators, lighting system, and so forth—are undoubtedly familiar enough to you. And Gooper has told me that you know all about artificial gravity—though I'm still waiting for an explanation of why you don't apply it, to commercial uses or to space-travel. But over here—come back into this room, please—is something that I'm pretty sure you *don't* know anything about." He beamed at Clair—this was the crowning achievement of their joint career.

"Right there. What we call the 'protolens.' That's the thing that focusses the force of protomagnetism on the tiny filament of—of an artificial element, atomic number 99. This element, like all the heavier ones, is—is like— " The word he had sought was 'radioactive,' but he fumbled in vain for the Gaylen equivalent. "Say, Art," he said in English, "what's Gaylen for radium?"

Clair was also stymied. "I don't know that I've ever heard it. Will you" (to the Gaylens) "supply us with your word meaning an element of such nature that its atoms break down, forming other elements of lesser atomic weight and giving off—giving off an emanation in the process?"

His hosts only looked blank. Ionic Intersection said, "On our world we have nothing of that nature."

Gaynor turned back to Clair. "How's that, Art? I thought radioactivity was an essential of every element."

"Well, in a way, yes," said his partner thoughtfully. "But only detectably in the very heavy ones. And—Art—now that you think of it, have you seen, or heard any of our pals mention any of the really heavy elements? I haven't—they don't even use mercury in their lab thermometers. Although it would be a lot more efficient and accurate than the thermocouples they do have."

"I see what you mean," Gaynor said excitedly. "All their heavy metals, being heavy and therefore radioactive, have broken down to the lighter ones. Why, Art, we're in an old universe!"

"Probably. Maybe just an old sun, though—after all, the development of an entire universe probably wouldn't be uniform. . . . So anyway, that might explain a lot of things about these Gaylens—why, with all their knowledge of science, they die like flies to carcinoma and other cancers, for instance. Maybe we've got something we can give them for a present, as a sort of payment for their saving our lives." He smiled amiably at Ionic Intersection as he spoke, and the girl, though not understanding a word of their jabber in a "foreign tongue," smiled back.

Gaynor scratched his head. To the Gaylens he

said, "This is going to take time to explain. More time than I'd figured, because this is *the* key-point of the structure of the *Prototype*. Let's step outside."

"I'll stay here," said Ionic Intersection. "Provided one of you will be so good as to show me the mechanical features of the ship. I'm not covering electronics any more—I decided to let someone else make a name for himself there."

"Very commendable," said Gaynor busily. "Jocelyn, point things out to the lady and see that nothing happens."

He, Clair, and the others filed out of the ship, and he leaned against the main door, swinging it shut, to continue his lecture.

"Unfortunately," he said, "I cannot demonstrate with a chunk of—of one of the elements I mean since we forgot to bring any along. But perhaps you have observed the phenomenon occasioned by the passing of an electric current through such inert gaseous elements as neon, argon, nitrogen, and so forth?"

"It is one of the most vexing riddles of our science," said one Gaylen.

"Well, that is a phenomenon closely allied with the force of which we spoke. The particles of the gases— " and he droned on, trying to explain the incomprehensible to the Gaylens. Gaynor could not stand still while speaking—a habit acquired in the lecture rooms of half-a-dozen universities, he had to walk back and forth. He did so now, but completed just one lap. For, as he, still talking, turned—

He saw the *Prototype* quietly, and as if by magic, vanish!

Somehow, surely inadvertently, possibly in trying to produce a sample of radioactive matter in the condensers, Jocelyn had allowed the ship to be dragged out of this good universe once more by the awful force of protomagnetism.

III. Nova!

The Gaylens looked about blankly. "What happened?" asked one of them dumbly.

"She started the ship!" choked Gaynor. "She's gone. God knows where or how!"

"Surely she can be traced," said Gooper sympathetically.

"How? There's no such thing as a tracer for the *Prototype*—it might be anywhere and anytime, in any dimension or frame of the cosmos."

Clair nodded numb affirmation.

One of the Gaylens coughed. "Then this is probably the best time to tell you . . ." he paused.

"Tell us what?" snapped Gaynor eagerly.

"Well—that you would be just as well off, in a way, if you were with your companion."

"I don't understand," said Gaynor, losing attention once more to the question of the whereabouts of Jocelyn and the *Prototype*.

"This planet will soon be unsuited to your temperament and physique," explained the Gaylen carefully.

"Stop beating around the bush," interjected Clair fiercely. "What's the secret?"

Gooper took over. "What he means," he said, "is that now we should tell you what we have successfully concealed from you for the duration of your stay—not wishing to inhibit your pleasure at again attaining security. In short . . . our sun is about to become a nova. Within a matter of days, as we calculate it, and this planet will be well within the orbit of the expanding photosphere."

Gaynor actually reeled with the shocking impact that the words carried.

"But you— " he said inarticulately. "What will happen to you?"

Gooper smiled. "Our bodies will perish."

"But what will happen to your civilization? Why— " he was struck by a sudden thought— "why

did you have us make a record for you—who is going
to use it after the nova comes?"

"We are not unprepared," said Gooper. "Don't
ask questions for a few seconds—come downstairs
with me."

En masse they descended, walking into a large,
bare room. Gooper proudly indicated a sort of pen
in the center.

"Behold!"

Gaynor looked over the little fence, and recoiled
at the horrors within. "What are they?" he gasped.
For he was looking at a dozen or more small things
that were at once slimy and calcined—like lizards,
save that lizards were at least symmetrical. That was
little to say of any animal, but certainly no more
could be said of lizards, and not even that of these
creatures. Blankly, he wondered how they could
have evolved to their present fantastic condition.

One of the Gaylens pressed a floor-stud, and
transparent shields slowly rose to curve about and
cover the pen completely.

"That area," said Gooper, "is now a refractory
furnace of the highest type, able to reproduce the
conditions that will obtain on this planet when the
nova occurs. Watch carefully."

Gaynor, in spite of himself, bent over the furnace as it slowly heated up. He shielded his eyes as
electric currents went into play and made the floor
within the pen white hot—and more. And still the
lizard-like creatures crawled sluggishly around the
sizzling floor, seemingly completely unaffected by
the heat!

Tongues of burning gas leaped out from the
shield, and the air became a blazing inferno within
the little confine of the pen. Obviously the shield
was an insulator of the highest type, and yet it slowly
reddened, and Gaynor backed cautiously away from
it, still observing the creatures.

"Watch!" cried Gooper tensely, pointing to one
of the creatures. It, completely oblivious to the heat,
was fumbling with a small pellet of something on

the floor—possibly food, Gaynor thought as he tried to make out, through the glare and burning gases, just what Gooper wanted him to observe. Then Gaynor noticed, and thought he was going mad. The thing picked up the pellet—it was food, of a sort, apparently—and put it in its mouth. And the organs with which it picked the pellet up were hands—tiny, glassy-scaled, perfectly formed human hands.

"Enough," said Gooper. And slowly the gas flame died down and the floor cooled. They retreated into the next room, and Gaynor faced his hosts in baffled wonder.

"Now will you tell me what was the purpose of that demonstration?" he demanded.

"No doubt you wondered about the evolution of those creatures," said a Gaylen obliquely. "It should soothe you to know that they're not natural—what with surgical manipulation of the embryos and even the ova of a species of lizard, we produced them artificially. You noted two great features—complete resistance to heat, and a perfect pair of hands—more than perfect, in fact, because they have two thumbs apiece, which your hands and ours don't."

"Yes," said Clair, "I noticed them. And a nasty shock they gave me, too. What are they for?"

"Well, you should have guessed—the nova is the reason. We've known it was coming for quite a while—more than a thousand years. And so long ago the cornerstone was laid for the edifice which you have just seen."

"If there is one thing more than another I hate about you Gaylens—outside of your habit of keeping facts like the approach of a nova from us—it's your longwindedness," said Clair angrily. "I want to know just what those hellish horned toads have to do with the nova."

The Gaylen coughed delicately. "A third feature of the creatures which could not be displayed to you is that their brains—note that I say nothing about their minds—their brains are fully as large, proportionately, and as well-developed, as ours and yours."

"And," Gooper interjected, "we have a gadget invented by my great grandfather, Parapsychic Transposition, which allows us to transfer mentalities between any two living things with brain-indices of higher rating than plus six.... Do you begin to follow?"

"I think so," said Gaynor slowly. "But get on!"

"So, when the nova bursts, we shall—all the Gaylens shall—each have his mind and memories and—I think your word for it is *psyche*— transferred into the body of one of those little animals. And— our civilization, though no longer human, perhaps, will go on."

Clair gasped. "What an idea!"

"Our only chance of survival."

Clair collapsed onto a seat. "Ye gods!" he cried accusingly. "And you didn't tell us before!"

"We thought you could leave at any moment— and, if not, there are more of the lizard-hosts than are necessary."

Clair thought of the things he had seen in the pen, reviewing their better points, trying to shut out the memory of their utter, blasphemous hideousness. He looked at Gaynor, obviously thinking the same thoughts. The look was enough. "Speaking for my partner and myself," he said to the Gaylens, "the answer is no. The flattest and most determined no you ever heard in your born days."

"Very well," said Gooper quietly. "Whatever you wish. But—the nova will be on us in a week."

IV. The Archetype

"How's chances, Pavel?" asked Clair grimly, looking about their borrowed lab.

"Well, small. Small, if you're refering to the chances of the late John L. Sullivan appearing before us in a cloud of glory. But if you mean of our finding

Jocelyn, or Jocelyn finding us—the chances are *real* small."

"That's about how I figured it," said his companion wearily. "Why even bother?"

"Earthman's burden, maybe. Anyway, the program is: first we manufacture some 99, then we make a protolens, then we build a ship around them. . . . How long did they say we had before this planet starts frying like henfruit on a griddle?"

"About a week. Is that plenty?"

"Well," said Gaynor soberly, "considering that it took us upwards of two years to finish the *Prototype*, when we had all the resources we needed, and enough radioactive substances to fill a pickle barrel, it isn't exactly too much time. Of course, we have the experience now."

"Right again," said Clair sullenly. "Doesn't it irritate you—this business of never being wrong?"

"Sorry, bud—it's the way I'm built. Like clockwork—you give me the data and I click out the answers, right every time. . . . Well, we seem to be missing just about everything. It will be sort of hard getting away from here without any sort of a ship. But does that stop the Rover Boys of space?"

"Yes," said Clair flatly. "Let's stop kidding ourselves. I'd sooner drink slow poison than have one of their psychotaxidermists put this nice brain of mine into one of those asbestos lizards. And I know like I know my own name that you would, too."

There was no answer to that. But Gaynor was spared the necessity of inventing one when the doorbell rang—just like on Earth. Eager for any distraction, he answered it.

Gooper stepped in, a rare smile on his face. "Greetings, friends," he said cheerily.

"Yeah?" growled Clair. "What are you happy about?"

"It's a fine day outside," said the Gaylen, "the air is bracing, all machinery's working beautifully—and we've worked out a solution to your particular problem."

"That so?" asked Gaynor. "What is it?"

"Wait a couple days and you'll see," said the Gaylen confidently. "We boys down at the Heavy Industries Trust want to surprise you."

"You might yell 'boo!' at us when we're not looking," said Gaynor sourly. "Nothing else could surprise us about you."

"I agree with my collaborator," confirmed Clair. "Go away, Gooper. And stay away until we send for you, please. We have a lot of heavy thinking to do."

"Oh, all right—if you want it that way," snapped Gooper, petulantly. He huffed out of the door, leaving the two Earthmen slumped despondently over a bench, thinking with such intensity that you could smell their short hairs frizzled with the heat.

Two days later they were still sitting, though they had stopped the flow of thought a few times for food, sleep, and the other necessities of the body.

"Art," said Clair.

"Yes?"

"Do you suppose that Gooper had the McCoy when he said that they'd solved our problem?"

"I doubt it. No good can come from a Gaylen— take that for an axiom."

"I know they've got bad habits. But where would we be if it weren't for them?"

"Are you glad you're here?" cried Gaynor savagely.

"Not very. But its better than lying poisoned in the Prototype. And their projector—the one they used to drag us in is a marvelous gadget—even you should admit that."

"Why?" asked Gaynor glumly.

"Because," said Clair complacently, "I just figured out an answer to our difficulties, and the projector forms a large part of it."

"Yeah?"

"Yeah! Because all we have to do is to coax the Gaylens into letting us have some sort of a shell—a boiler or a water-tank will do, if it's gas-tight—and then fix it up for living purposes." Clair sat back triumphantly.

"And what good does that do us? We can't stay in it forever, if that's what you're driving at—even if we could get one that was a good enough insulator to keep out the heat."

"Far from it. I examined their traction-projectors, and learned how to work them. They're a good deal like our own artificial-gravity units, which, you may remember, are now floating around in the *Prototype* somewhere. Only these things are powered by electricity, and they don't require a great deal of that, either. I've been trying to dope out just how they work, but I haven't got very far, and Gooper keeps referring me to the experts in the field whenever I ask him. But I can handle them all right, so if we stick a quartz window in the shell, and install the projector, and seal it up nice and tidy—"

"We can take off!" yelled Gaynor. "Art, you have it!" He whooped with joy. "We can tack out into space— "

"Head for the nearest star— "

"Raise our own garden truck with hydroponics— "

"Maybe locate some radium— "

"Live long and useful lives until we do— "

"And if not, what the hell!" finished Gaynor.

"So we'll call up Gooper and have it done." Clair began punching the combination of wall-studs that customarily sent their host and name-sake dashing into the room, but for once he actually preceded the summons.

"Something I want to show you," he said as he entered.

"Lead on," said Clair exuberantly, and all together they mounted the moving ramp. Clair began to describe his brainchild.

But halfway through Gooper stamped his foot and uttered an impatient exclamation.

"What's the matter?" asked Clair, surprised. "Won't it work?"

"We wanted to surprise you," said Gooper mournfully. "Remember?"

"Distinctly. But where is this surprise?"

"Here," said Gooper as they dismounted, leading the way into a room of colossal proportions. And there on the floor, looking small amid its surroundings, but bulking very large beside the hundred-odd men who were tinkering with it, was the very image of Clair's machine—a mammoth ex-steam boiler, fitted with quartz ports and a gastight door, containing full living quarters, supplies, and a gravity projector.

Clair and Gaynor staggered back in mock astonishment. "Pavlik," said Clair gravely. "I like their system of production here. No sooner does one dream up a ship than its on the ways and ready to be launched."

"Let's look the blighter over," said Gaynor. "What shall we call it?"

"*Archetype*," said Clair instantly. "The primitive progenitor of all space ships. *Archie* for short."

"Not *Archie*," said Gaynor, making a mouth of distaste. "No dignity there. How about calling it the Ark?"

"That'll do. *Archetype* she is, now and forever more." They entered the capacious port and looked cautiously around.

"Big, isn't it?" Gaynor commented superfluously.

"Very big. Hydroponics tanks and everything. Stores and spare parts too."

"We left little to chance," said Gooper proudly. "This may be the last job of engineering of any complexity that our people will do for some time, so we made it good and impressive, both. I don't see how, outside of diving into the sun, you can manage to get hurt in this thing."

"What are those?" suddenly asked Clair, pointing to a brace of what looked like diving suits.

"In case you want to explore our unaffected planet," said Gooper.

"Are there any?" cried Gaynor, his eyes popping.

"Only one. It will be well out of the danger zone. You can even settle the Ark there if you like, instead of living in space. Its gravity is a bit high, but not too much so."

"Look, Gooper," broke in Clair. "I just had a simply marvelous idea."

"What is it?" asked the Gaylen with suspicious formality.

"You have a bit of time left. If you work hard, enough time to fabricate more of these ships, to transport a lot of your people to that planet. Why not do it? You probably couldn't get all of them there in time, but a good nucleus, say, for development."

Gooper scratched his head thoughtfully. "Psychologies differ," he said finally. "And we stand in utter terror of space travel. We would sooner go through the fantastic hells of our ancient religious ancestors than venture outside the atmosphere. Without a doubt this has cost us much in knowledge we might have gained—but some things are unaccountable, and this is one of them, I suppose. Do you understand?"

"No," said Gaynor bluntly. "But I don't suppose there's much need to understand. It's a fact, and it's there. Well, there's an end. When can we take off?"

"Right now, if you wish," said the Gaylen. He gestured at a control man high in a little box stuck to one of the transparent walls, and slowly the mighty vaulted roof of the place split and began to roll back. "Just turn on the power and you'll flit away from the planet," he said. "After that, you're on your own."

V. The Proteans

"It is bigger than I thought," said Clair absently, staring through the port of the Ark.

"Mean the planet?" asked Gaynor.

"What else, ape? Do we land?"

"I suppose so." Gaynor peered down at the mighty world spinning slowly beneath them.

"Then the question is—how?"

"Find a nice soft spot and let go," suggested Gaynor. "Anyway, you're the navigator. You dope it out."

In answer, his companion sent the ship into a vicious lurch that spilled Gaynor out of the hammock into which he had just crawled. "Necessary maneuver," he explained genially.

"Necessary like a boil behind the ear," grunted Gaynor. "Let me take over."

Lazily they drifted down for a short period, then came to a near halt, perhaps five thousand feet above the ground, settled, fell again, halted; settled again, fell, and landed with a shattering jolt.

"Very neat, pal," said Clair with disgust oozing from his tones. "Very neat."

"I could do better with the practice," said Gaynor diffidently. "Do you want I should go up again and come down again maybe?"

"Heaven forbid!" said Clair hastily. "Let's get out and case the joint."

They donned fur garments thoughtfully laid out by one of the nameless builders of the Ark and stepped through the port. Clair took one deep breath and choked inelegantly. "Smells like the back room of McGuire's Bar and Grill," he said, burying his nostrils in his furs.

"How does the gravity strike you, Art?" said Gaynor.

"Easy, Pavlik, easy. A little heavier than is conducive to comfort, but agreeable in many ways. It seems to be dragging yesterday's dinner right out of my stomach, but it's not too bad. How's for you?"

"I feel sort of light in the head and heavy everywhere else. But I can thrive on anything that doesn't knock you for a loop."

"See any animal life?"

"Not yet. The Gaylens didn't mention any, did they?"

"No. But they couldn't—all they know about any of their planetary brethren is what they can see at long range," said Clair.

"True for you, Art. Now, what would you call *this*?" As he spoke Gaynor pulled from the flint-hard soil a thing that seemed a cross between planet and animal. It looked at him glumly, squeaked once, and died.

"Possibly you've slain a member of the leading civilization of this globe," said Clair worriedly.

"I doubt that. You don't find advancement coupled with soil-feeding."

"There's another reason why this thing isn't the leading representative of the life of this planet," said Clair, staring weakly over Gaynor's shoulder. "Unless they built it, which I don't believe."

Gaynor spun around and stared wildly. It was a city, a full-fledged metropolis which had sprung up behind his back. It was—point for point and line for line—the skyline of New York.

Then the city got up and began to walk toward them with world-shaking strides.

"You mean the city with *legs*?" Gaynor cried, beginning to laugh hysterically.

"My error," said Clair elaborately, passing a hand before his eyes. "I mean the giraffe."

Gaynor looked again, and where the city had been was now a giraffe. It looked weird and a trifle pathetic ambling across the flinty plain. It seemed to be having more than a little trouble in coordinating its legs.

"Must be an inexperienced giraffe," muttered Gaynor. "No animal that knew what it was doing would walk like that."

"You're right," said Clair vaguely. "But you can't blame it. It hasn't been a giraffe very long, and it wants practice. What next, do you suppose?"

"Possibly a seventy-ton tank." And the moment the words left Gaynor's mouth he regretted them. For the giraffe dwindled into a tiny lump, and then the lump swelled strangely and took shape, becoming just that—a seventy-ton tank, half a mile away, bearing down on them with murder and sudden death in its every line and curve.

Within a couple of yards of the humans the tank dwindled again to a thing more like a whale than anything else in the travelers' pretty wide experience—but with some features all of its own.

"Hello," said Gaynor diffidently, for lack of something more promising to say or do.

And a mouth formed in the prow of the creature. "Hello," responded the mouth.

"I presume you're friendly," said Gaynor, drawn and mad. "At lease, I hope so."

"Quite friendly," said the mouth. "Are you?"

"Oh, quite," cried Gaynor enthusiastically, sweat breaking forth on his brow. "Is there anything I can do for you to prove it?"

"Yes," said the mouth. "Go away."

"Gladly," said Gaynor. "But there are reasons for us being here— "

"Do they really matter?" asked the mouth. "To a Protean, I mean."

"To a what?"

"To a Protean. That, I deduce from your rather disgusting language, is what you would eventually come to call me, from my protean powers of changing shape. That's what I am—a Protean, probably the highest form of life in this or any universe."

"You're a little flip for a very high form of life," muttered Clair sullenly.

"I learned it from you, after all, the whole language. And naturally I learned your little 'flip' tricks of talking. Would you like a demonstration of my practically infinite powers—something to convince you?"

"Not at all necessary," interrupted Gaynor hastily. "I—we believe you. We'll leave right away."

"No," said the Protean. "You can't, and you

know you can't. Moreover, while it is certain that your presence here disturbs me and my people with your very sub-grade type of thought, we have so constituted ourselves that we are merciful to a fault. If we weren't we'd blast the planet to ashes first time we got angry. I want to do you both a favor. What shall it be?"

"Well," brooded Gaynor, "there's a woman at the bottom of it all."

"Females again!" groaned the Protean. "Thank God we reproduce by binary fission! But go on—sorry I interrupted."

"Her name is Jocelyn, and she's lost."

"Well?" demanded the mouth.

"Well what?"

"Shall I see that she stays lost or do you want her to be found?"

"Found, by all means found!" cried Gaynor.

"Thanks. Wait for me." Then the Protean vanished for a moment and became a perfect duplicate in size and scale of the Ark. Then it flashed up and out of sight.

VI. New Sun—and Old

Gaynor stared at Clair—stared at him hard. Then he coughed. With a start his partner came to. "Anything wrong, Paul?" he asked soberly.

"Anything wrong. Anything wrong," murmured Gaynor quietly, almost to himself. Then he exploded, "Art, you bloody idiot, don't you realize that we were in the presence of a Protean—the mightiest organism of any time or space? It even admits it—it must be so!"

"I'm sorry, Paul," said Clair gently. "But I was busy with a theory. I noticed something, yes, but it didn't seem terribly important at the time. What happened to the giraffe we were talking to?"

Gaynor choked. It was rarely that this happened—but when it did something usually came of it. The first of these near-trances he had witnessed had come when Clair, in the middle of the Nobel Prize award, had glazed his eyes and stood like a log, leaving Gaynor to make a double speech of acceptance. And all the way back to America he had been in a trance, mumbling vaguely when spoken to, or not answering at all.

A dot appeared in the sky—two dots. As they swooped down Gaynor recognized, with a jumping heart, the *Prototype* being towed by what looked like the *Archetype*, but really was, of course, the Protean who had forced the favor on him.

Gently they landed, almost at his feet. And then the *Ark* turned into the whale-like creature again, and the mouth remarked, "Is there anything else I can do for you?"

"Yes. How do we get back to Earth?"

"Ha!" laughed the creature. "You can think up some funny ones. Please visualize the planet for my benefit. I'll have to explore your mind a little for this. Have I your permission to do so?"

"Certainly!" cried Gaynor.

"Thank you," said the Protean, as the man began to concentrate on the more salient features of his native planet.

"I said thank you," repeated the creature to the expectantly waiting Gaynor. "It's all over. You didn't have too much of a mind to explore."

Gaynor was disappointed—the Gaylen mind-teachers had been a lot more spectacular, and a *lot* less insulting. "Well," he asked, "funny as it may seem to you, how do we get back to the place?"

"You know already," said the Protean. "At least, your colleague does. Why don't you ask him? Now will you leave?"

"Certainly," said Gaynor, puzzled but eager. "And all our thanks to you for your kindness."

"Just being neighborly," said the Protean. Whereupon it dwindled into a tiny worm-like thing

which slipped down an almost imperceptible hole
in the ground.

Gaynor looked blankly at Clair, wondering how
best to broach the subject of getting back, but, before
he could inaugurate a campaign to return the mental
marvel to the world of cold realities, the door of the
Prototype swung open wide, and Jocelyn Earle
stepped out.

"The trip didn't do you any good," said Gaynor, inspecting her face. "Whose idea was it?"

"Are you being stern, Pavlik?" she asked, flinging herself into his arms. When they had disentan-
gled she explained, indicating Ionic Intersection who
stood smiling in the doorway, "Her idea, really—she
couldn't stomach the idea of turning into a lizard to
avoid the nova. She even preferred floating around
in space—have you heard about the creeping quivers
that space travel gives these sissified Gaylens?—
well, she was even willing to face that instead."

"I felt," explained Ionic Intersection, "that I
have something to live for now, since—well, something to live for. And I find that space travel isn't
fractionally as bad as I'd expected—I almost like it
now, in a way."

As if to punctuate her sentence, Jocelyn emitted
a yelp. "Ye gods and little fishes!" she screamed.
"Look at the sun!"

The others looked—it was worth looking at.
Probably no human had ever seen a sun like that
before at closer range than half a thousand parsecs—
and lived. Great gouts of flame, and relatively min-
iature new suns composed of pure, raw, naked energy were spouting from it; rapidly and violently the
heat and light from it were increasing, becoming un-
comfortable even on this distant planet. It was becoming a nova by cosmic leaps and vast bounds.

"This is no place for us, friends—not while
we've got what it takes to get away. So let's go—fast.
I wouldn't put it past our Gaylen pals—with all due
respect to you, Ionic Intersection—to have forgotten

a decimal point or neglected a surd in their calculations. This planet may be as safe as they claimed— or it may not. I don't choose to take chances."

Shooing the ladies along ahead of him, Gaynor gently took Clair's elbow and walked him into the *Prototype*. "He's got a theory," he explained to the girls, neither of whom had ever seen him that way before. "It gets him at times like these, always. You'll have to bear with him; it's just another reason why he shouldn't marry."

Once they were all arranged in the *Prototype* and sufficient stores had been transferred from the *Archetype*, left to rust or melt on the planet of the Proteans, they took off and hovered in space far away from the wild sun.

"Now," said Gaynor, "we'll go home." So speaking, he took Clair by the arm once more, shaking him gently. "Theory-Protean-idea-home-*theory*-HOME!" he whispered in the entranced one's ear, in a sharp crescendo.

Clair came out of it with a start. "Do you know," he said quickly, "I've found the governing principle of our little mishaps and adventures?"

"Yes," said Gaynor, "I know. The Protean told me. He also told me that you knew how to apply that principle so as to get us home."

"Oh, yes. *Home*. Well, in order to get us home, I'll need your cooperation—all of your cooperation. I'll have to explain.

"I said a while ago that nothing was liable to hurt us in this universe. Well, nothing is. And the reason is that every stick, stone, proton, and mesotron in this universe is so placed and constructed that we *can't* get hurt. Don't interrupt—it's true. Listen.

"Let me ask a rhetorical question: How many possible universes are there? Echo answers: Plenty. An infinity of them, in fact. And the funny thing about it is that they all exist. You aren't going to argue that, are you, Paul? Because everybody knows that, in eternity, everything that is possible happens at least once, and the cosmos is eternal. . . . I thought you'd see that.

"There being so many universes, and there being no directive influence in the Prototype, there is absolutely no way of knowing, mathematically a provable point, just which universe we'll land in. But there has to be some determining factor, unless the law of cause-and-effect is meaningless, and all of organized science is phoney from the ground up.

"Well, there is a determining factor. It's—thought.

"Thought isn't very powerful, except when applied through such an instrument as the human mind, or rather through such a series of step-up transformers as the mind, the brain, the body, and the machines of humanity. But there are so many possible continua that even the tiny, tiny pressure of our thought-waves is plenty to decide which.

"What did we want before we hit the universe of the Gaylens? I don't know exactly what was in your minds, but I'll bet it was: food, human companionship, supplies, and SAFETY. And we got all of them.

"So—the rest becomes obvious. To get home: Think of home, all of us, each preferably picking a different and somewhat unusual object to concentrate upon, so as to limit the number of possible universes that fit the description—you, Ionic, will try not to think of anything, because you come from a different universe; then throw in the switch to the protolens—you're home."

They had made five false starts, and had spent a full week in one deceptive home-like universe before they'd got the correct combination of factors to insure a happy landing, but this one indubitably was it.

Clair was at the controls—had been for days of searching, and now that they had identified their solar system was driving every fragment of power from the artificial-gravity units.

Jocelyn and Gaynor approached him with long, sad faces. "Well, kiddies?"

"I love Jocelyn," said Gaynor unhappily.

"So," he said, not taking his eyes from the plate which mirrored stars and sun.

"And that's not the worst of it," said the girl directly. "I love Pavlik, too. Do you mind?"

"Bless you, my children," said Clair agreeably.

"But don't you *mind*?" cried Jocelyn indignantly. "We want to get married."

"A splendid idea. I'm all for marriage, personally."

"Good!" said Jocelyn heartily, though a bit puzzled and annoyed. "What you ought to do is to find some nice girl who can cook and sew and marry her."

"Impossible," said Clair.

"Why?"

"My wife wouldn't let me. Ionic Intersection. We were married three days ago."

"What!" shrieked Jocelyn, and Gaynor cried,

"You can't have been. We've been in space!"

"Sure. That's what made it so easy. You know the old law—the captain of a ship at sea can perform marriages."

"But— "

"But nothing. I'm the captain, and I performed the marriage—to me."

Gaynor reeled and clutched at a railing. "But—but since when are you captain—who appointed you?"

"Ha!" crowed Clair. "Shows how little you know about sea law. It's just like the case of a derelict—when the regular offficers and crew of a ship are unable to bring her to port—and you were definitely unable so to do—anyone who can takes command. That's the law, and I'm sticking to it. And you'd better not question it—because if you do, I'll dissolve your marriage."

"Our marriage! *What* marriage?" cried Jocelyn, incredulity and delight mingling in her voice.

"The one I performed over you two not five minutes ago. Probably you thought I was whistling through my teeth," Clair very patiently explained. "*Now* are there any objections?"

No, there were no objections. . . .

THE EXTRAPOLATED DIMWIT

I.

"I always smoke Valerons," declared Gaynor. "I have found that for the lift you need when you need it, they have no equal. Unreservedly I recommend them to all dimensional flyers and time-travelers." He gagged slightly and wiped his mouth. "Was that right?" he asked the ad man.

"Okay," said Alec Andrews of Dignam and Bailey, promoters. He disconnected the recording apparatus. "Mr. Gaynor," he declared fervently, "you will hear that every hour, on the hour, over the three major networks. And now ... ah ..." He took a checkbook from his pocket.

"Fifteen gees," said Gaynor happily, flipping a bit of paper between his fingers. "This, my pretty, will net you a fishskin evening gown."

"Yeah," said Jocelyn. "If I can keep you from buying a few more tons of junk for your ruddy lab."

Gaynor looked uneasy. "Hola, Clair," he greeted the wilted creature who entered, tripping over a wire.

"Hola yourself," muttered Clair disentangling. "I got it. All of it."

Jocelyn, tall, slim, cameolike, and worried, asked him: "Measles?"

"Nope. Differentiator Compass in six phases— just finished it. Creditors on my heels—needed two ounces of radium. Save me, Pavlik! Save your bosom friend!" He turned as a thundering noise indicated either his creditors or a volcano in eruption. "Here they are!" he groaned, diving under a table. Gaynor and his wife hastily arranged themselves before it as the door burst in.

It was a running argument between a plump little brunette and a crowd of men with grim, purposeful faces. "Gentlemen," she was saying with what dignity she could, "I've already told you that my husband has left suddenly for Canada to see his father. How can you ruthlessly desecrate this home with your yammerings for money— "

"Look, lady," said a hawk-eyed man. "We sold your husband that equipment in good faith. If he don't propose to settle for it now, we're just naturally going to slap a lawsuit on his hide."

"Hold it," interjected Gaynor. "Io, what's the damage?"

The plump woman sighed. "Thirty-five thousand. I told him he didn't need all that radium, Paul. What do we do now?"

Martyr-like, Gaynor unfolded the adman's check and endorsed it to cash. Jocelyn, beside him, took a deep breath and snarled wordlessly. "Here's something on account," he said, tendering it to the hawk-eyed creditor. "Come around for the rest in a week. Okay with you?"

"Okay, mister," said the hawk, handing over a receipt. "If your friend was more like you, us entrepreneurs'd have a lot easier time of it." He bowed out with his allies. Io closed the door and locked it.

"Now, Arthur," she began dangerously, "come out with your hands up!" She stared coldly as her husband, the distrait Clair, emerged from under the table. "Dearest," he began meekly.

"Don't you 'dearest' me," she spat. "If she weren't in another dimension and turned into a little leather slug, I'd go home to mother. Now explain youself!"

"Ah—yes," said Clair. "About that money. I'm sorry you had to turn over that check, Paul. But this thing I've finished—absolutely the biggest advance in spaceflight and transplanar navigation since the *proto*. The perfect check and counter-check on position. It's like the intention of the compass and sextant was to seamanship and earthly navigation."

"Well, what is it?" exploded Jocelyn.

"The Six-Phase Differentiator Compass, Jos. You see it here." He took from his breast pocket a little black thing like a camera or exposure meter. "Allow me to explain:

"This dingus, if I may call it such, is a permanent focus upon whatever it is permanently focused on. It acts like a Geiger counter in that when you approach the thing it was focused on, it ticks or buzzes. And the nearer you get, the louder it buzzes— or ticks. That is the tracer unit. And the other half of the gadget, the really complicated half that took all that radium, is a sort of calculating device. Like a permanent statistical table, but with a difference.

"Inside this case there is a condition of unique stress obtaining under terrific conditions of heat, radiation, bombardment, pressure, torsion, implosion, expansion, everything. And there is in there one little chunk of metal—a *cc* of lead it happens to be—that is taking all the punishment.

"Geared on to this *cc* of lead are a number of fairly delicate meters and reaction fingers—one for each dimension in which we navigate, making seven in all. From these meters you get a coordinate reading which will establish your position anywhere in the universe and likewise, if you set the dials for desired coordinates, it works in reverse and you have the processive matricies required. How do you like that?"

"Do you really want to know?" demanded Gaynor.

Clair nodded eagerly.

"I think it's the craziest mess of balderdash that's ever been dreamed up. I don't see how it can work or why you've been wasting your time and my money on it. Straight?"

Clair wilted. "Okay, Paul," he said. "You'll see." He drifted from the room, moping.

"Now where do you suppose he's going?" asked his wife.

"To get plastered, dear," replied Jocelyn.

"This," said Gaynor, "is a helluva way to make a living." He gestured with distaste at the stage waiting for him, and winced as the thunderous applause beat at his ears.

"Bend over," said Jocelyn.

"What for?" he demanded, bending, then yelped as his wife gave him a hearty kick in the pants. "Now why— " he began injuredly . . .

"Old stage tradition. Good luck. Now go out and give your little lecture. And make it good, because if you don't, there won't be any more little lectures and the creditors will descend on poor Ionic Intersection like a pack of wolves for what that louse of a husband she has owes them."

"I wish you wouldn't talk that way about Clair," complained Gaynor. "What if he has deserted the girl? Maybe she snores." He strode out onto the platform briskly and held up his hands to quiet the applause. "Thank you," he said into the mike. There was no amplification. He gestured wildly to the soundman who was offstage at his panels. "Hook me up, you nincompoop!"

The last word bellowed out over the loudspeakers. Gaynor winced. "Excuse me, friends," he said, "that was wholly unpremeditated. Anyway, you're here to see the lantern-slides and hear my commentary. Well—let's have Number One, Mr. Projectionist."

A lantern slide flashed onto the screen as the hall darkened. "There you see me and my partner,

Art Clair, directly after we received the Nobel Prize. Suffice to say that it took us a week to learn that you can't drink Akvavit, the national potion of Norway, like water, or even gasoline. The best way to handle the stuff is to place a bowl of it at a distance of fifteen feet and lie down in a padded room where you aren't likely to hurt yourself when you advance into the spastic stage of an Akvavit jag. Note the bruises on Mr. Clair's jaw. He thought he was saying 'Thank you' in Norwegian. He wasn't. Next!

"This fetching creature on the screen is Miss Jocelyn Earle, at the time of the picture, a reporter for the *Helio*. She was given the assignment, one sunshiny day, of investigating the work in progress of those two lovable madcaps, Gaynor and Clair. Fool that she was, she accepted it. She found that the work in progress consisted of a little thing known as the *Prototype*, whose modest aim was to transmit Art and me to the beginning of the universe. This it did, but with a difference. Jocelyn came too.

"Now you see the *Prototype*, all forty feet of it. I won't go into the details of construction and theory; suffice to say that it worked, and you see—get it up, Mr. Projectionist!—a porthole view of things as they were about eleven skillion years ago, before the planets, before the stars, before, even, the nebulae. By this time, Art and I were desperately in love with Miss Earle. Despite her obvious physical charms, we discovered on that journey that she was a woman of much brain-capacity, besides cooking up the best dish of beans that side of eternity. Next!

"Observe the pixies. I don't expect you to believe me, but after the *Prototype* got out into the primordial state before the nebulae, we were chased by, in rapid succession, flying dragons, pixies, and a planet with a mouth. Eggs for the Alimentary Asteroid, as it were.

"Following this unhappy circumstance, we went through some very trying times. The ship drifted for weeks, nearly out of fuel, and almost wholly out of control. Things were in a very sad way until—next!—a greenish sort of glow filled the ship and we found ourselves on the planet of the Gaylens, not much the worse for wear.

"These Gaylens were a charming but absent-minded people of a peculiarly lopsided kind of scientific development. They were just about precisely like us, human physically and very nearly so psychologically.

"Comes nova. Mr. Projectionist, will you change that damn slide?" A view of a tropical island flashed onto the screen. "Cut out the horseplay!" Gaynor bawled. The tropical island vanished and a terrific view of a nova sun appeared. "That's better, thanks.

"These Gaylens changed themselves into little leather slugs to live during the nova. This, Art, Jocelyn, and I couldn't stand. So they kindly whipped up for us a spaceship—we couldn't use the Prototype because Jocelyn and a Gaylen girl named Ionic Intersection—the Gaylens name themselves according to their work; this gal had developed something terrific in the way of Ionic Intersections and thus the odd-sounding name for her—had gone off with it by accident—and sent us off to another of their planets. Next!"

A view of sunset over Pearl Harbor, Hawaii, appeared. Gaynor muttered a curse. "Bud, if you want me to climb your crow's-nest and break your neck, I'll do it. Let's have that Protean before I hurt you!" The sunset yielded to an immense whale-like creature glancing coyly out of the corner of its seven eyes. "Okay, Mr. Projectionist, I'll see you later.

"That big thing is a Protean, the highest form of life in that or any other universe, I suspect. They live a completely mental existence, and their only wish is not to be bothered by Outsiders. And as such we qualified, for theirs was the planet on which we landed. Anyway they did us a favor—or rather, this particular Protean did—by finding Jocelyn, Ionic Intersection, and the Prototype for us, dragging them back from some God-forsaken corner of creation.

Then he sped us on our merry way with the blessings of his tribe on our heads and the heartfelt wish that we'd come back no more.

"Once out in space and time in the Prototype, we had yet to find our way home. And that, to make a long story short, was by intellectual means. By a kind of mental discipline we were able to preselect our landing place and time. Anyway, my friend Clair had somewhere forgotten that he was madly in love with Miss Earle and had gone overboard for Miss Intersection, a pretty brunette, it turns out. Next!

"Here you see a wedding group. Being captain of the ship, I was empowered to perform marriages, of course. So it was a double wedding. Miss Earle is now Mrs. Gaynor, and Miss Intersection is now Mrs. Clair, much to her regret. Next!

"A scenic shot of our welcoming committee, including the mayor and other notables. Art is holding the key to the city. We tried to hock it, later. No go."

The sceen went blank and the house lights on. "To complete the story," said Gaynor gently, "I need only add that two weeks ago Art Clair vanished with the look of liquor in his eyes and has not been seen since. Thank you one and all." He bowed himself from the stage to thunderous applause.

"Nice work," said Jocelyn. "A few more like that and maybe we'll be able to pay off." Ionic Intersection bustled up. "Jos," she said worriedly, extending a note, "what does this say? I think it's from Art. He's been home then gone to the lab. He left the note home, but when I got to the lab he was gone. Everything was messed up."

Gaynor took the note. "Lemme see." He whistled as he read. "Io, your husband's done a very rash thing. Listen:

> Dear kids:
> In spite of your unflattering opinions I still
> have reason to suspect that I know more than

a little science in my field. In proof whereof I submit that you will find the Six-Phase Integrated Analyser—I like that better than Differential Compass—in my desk drawer. To make a long story short, I've hopped off in *Proto, Jr.*, the little experimental one-man ship.

And I'm going to get myself thoroughly lost in time, space, and dimensions—as much so as is humanly possible. I don't want to be able to get back of my own free will. This, chums, is so you will just have to find me—and to find me you'll have to use the much-derided Analyser. Okay?

Love.
Art.

Gaynor stared about him. "That dope," he said to the world at large. "How do you like that?"

Ionic Intersection was weeping softly. "What are we going to do?" she asked.

"Just wait around, dear," said Jocelyn. "He'll probably come back with a wild tale or two. Right, Paul?"

"Wrong," said her husband incisively. "He meant what he said. We'd better outfit the *Prototype* for an extended journey. The *Proto Jr.* doesn't hold enough air, water, and food for more than a few days. And I hope he won't be late. This is what comes of forming an alliance with a ringtailed baboon."

"Don't you say that about my husband!" objected Io. "He just wants to show that his tracer works."

"Yeah. And if it doesn't, I'll be minus a partner and you'll be minus a husband. Come on; we're off!"

II.

The *Prototype* loomed on the colossal floor of the lab like a big silver fish, slick with oil. Gaynor shuddered. "That baboon— " he muttered incontinently.

"Okay, kids, we're ready for the happy journey. Pile in." He inspected the tracing compass and held it to his ear. "Just barely sounding," he mused worriedly. "It's below the estimated level of perception. I suspect that our mutual friend has kept his promise and is very lost indeed."

He climbed into the ship and sealed the rubber-lipped bulkhead. "Anteros, here we come," he sighed, flinging down the lever of the protolens. There was a soft, slipping moment of transition that they could all recognize so well, and then through the port blinked countless stars in strange configurations. "Now," said Gaynor, "where do you suppose we are?"

"Looks normal," said Jocelyn. "But the constellations are all out of whack, of course. What do we do now?"

Her husband put the tracer to his ear. "The very faintest kind of buzzing. This isn't the time, space, or plane of perception we want. But we'd better look around, anyway." He shot the *Prototype* at a sun. "We'll level out the curve of trajectory about a million miles from the troposphere," he explained, twiddling with the controls, "and ride on energy. Like a switchback. Only—" the twiddling had become desperate—"we don't seem to be able to level out. In fact, we're about to plunge into that sun!"

"Awk!" gulped Jocelyn. "What'll it be like?"

"Instant annihilation after a brief moment of intense discomfort," replied her husband, abandoning the controls and leaning back in the bucket seat. "Kiss me, sweet."

Jocelyn kissed him clingingly as they drove into the terrible, blazing surface of the sun. Then she looked at him coldly. "Well, when do we die?"

He looked baffled. "A few seconds ago. A glance will show you that we are in the center of a very big star and are even now emerging without any damage to the ship or to us. I submit that the star is cold. And why that should be, I'm damned if I know."

"Yew brat!" snapped a sharp, bitter voice. "Will

yew git ter tarnation gone out of my universe or dew
I have ter kick ye out?"

"Who's that?" asked Jocelyn.

"Davy Canter, thet's who!" snapped back the
irritable voice. "This is my universe and I ain't hank-
erin' after intruders. Ef'n yew-all want ter see me
face ter face, I'm on the seventh planet of thet sun
yew jest ran through. And ef'n yer comin', come and
ef'n yer gittin', git!"

"Sounds like an invitation," said Gaynor mildly.
"Shall we call?" He selected the seventh planet and
roared over its surface. The one huge continent that
made it up was covered with ruins—and the most
godawful ruins that anyone had ever seen anywhere.
Periods and styles of architecture were jumbled close
together; a Norman tower mouldering chock-by-jowl
with a dilapidated super-city of shining concrete and
glass met their eyes. Fascinated, they stared, as much
at the scene as at the figure of the black-bearded
hillbilly, complete with shotgun, standing atop a
tower.

"Yew head north," came the voice. "Jest land
in a clear bit o' land and I'll be there."

"Okay," said Gaynor helplessly. He landed the
ship and opened the port. The wild-eyed backwoodsman confronted him, shotgun raised. "I'm Davy Canter," said the woodsman through his disheveled
whiskers. "An' I dont see why folks cain't leave folks
alone when they wants ter be alone. Whut do ye want
in my universe?"

"Sorry, Mr. Canter," said Gaynor diplomati-
cally. "I'm Paul Gaynor."

The backwoodsman stared at him in glee and
cackled cheerfully. "Yew must be the fella that Billikin was always a-cussin' up n' daown," he said.
"I'm right pleased ter meet up with yew." He extended his hand and solemnly they shook. Gaynor
introduced the ladies and invited Canter in for a
smoke and chat.

"Thank ye kindly," said the backwoodsman,
who seemed to be warming up to them. "I reckon

ye're wondering how come I got myself a universe all my own, hey?"

"Indeed we are," said Jocelyn. "It looks like a good trick."

"I'll begin at the beginnin'," said Canter comfortably. "I was known as the hermit of Razorback Crag back in West Virginia when this here Billikin, who said as haow he wuz a scientist feller, come to my place. He said he'd be gone in a little while ef'n I let him have the run o' the cabin n' creek, and fust of all, he works up a batch o' corn likker thet gits me jest warm with admiration—so I let him stay. All the time he was a-cussin Gaynor and Clair fer fakers and cheats, talkin' like a tetched man.

"He sets him up a lot of machinery on top of the Crag with storage batteries and things and finally says to me: 'Davy,' he says, 'I'm agoin' to fix them two fakers, Gaynor n' Clair. I'm agoin' to build a universe all my own. An' so help me ef'n they ever come traipsin' into it, I'm jes' nacherally agoin' ter shoot them dead fer trespassin'.' Then he pulls a switch an falls doawn daid. I guess it wuz heart failure or somethin'; he wuz as old as the hills. I looks him over 'n' takes a little swig o' thet corn—'n' then I reckon as haow I must have fell agin' another switch because I foun' myself afloatin' in space. So I sez to myself, I wish as haow I wuz on solid graound, and by ganny, I am! Then I sez to myself, I wish they wuz a sun up thar in the sky, and by ganny there is!

"So I bin here two or three years, I reckon, and, fuddlin' araound, buildin' cities and reducin' them agin, puttin' stars in the sky an' takin' them out when I get tired o' them. It's a sort o' lonely life, Mister Gaynor, an' ladies, but I wuz a hermit before Billikin came an' I guess he just sort of expanded my career, you might say."

"Extraordinary!" breathed Jocelyn.

"Thank yew, ma'am," said the hermit, staring at her with unconcealed curiosity. "An' naow, seein' ez haow I've told yew-all my story, mebbe yew can be atellin' me yours?"

"Nothing very much to it, Mr. Canter," said Gaynor. "This other egg, Clair, that Billikin was cursing up and down along with me, got himself lost in a universe of his own, I suspect. Only where it is, we don't know, and he hasn't got air and water enough to last him more than a couple of days. And, unfortunately, his universe probably isn't as convenient as yours, what with providing him with whatever he wishes for."

"Sho is a pity," mused Davy, shaking his head wisely. "Mebbe yew'd better push off, seein' as haow yer friend's stuck. But befo' yo-all git, ah'd mightly like fo' yew ter sample maw corn. Would yew be interested? Ah bin wishin' thet kind thet Billikin cooked up for me fust of all—sho' is fine likker, mister."

"Indeed, I would like some," said Gaynor, interrupting Jocelyn. They exchanged murderous glances. Davy cackled and produced a jug and glasses from his vest pocket. "Try this," he offered, pouring three and one with the authentic backwoods overhand spill.

"Thanks," said Gaynor gulping. "Awk!" he shrilled a second later. "*Water!*"

Davy was undisturbed. He waved his hand in a vague sweep and there was a firehose in it, whose tube snaked far back into the tumbled horizon. He played the terrific blast upon Gaynor, drenching him thoroughly. "Thet enough?" he asked, vanishing the hose.

Gaynor looked at him without words, wringing out his tie.

"Thanks," said Jocelyn, grinning. She set down her glass untasted, and promptly it vanished. "But now we really must be going."

"Well—seein' ez ye must, ye must," said the hermit. "But it wuz sort of nice fer ye ter drop in on a lonely old man."

"Davy!" shrilled a voice. The voyagers looked

through the door. A sweet, round young thing in brightly checked gingham was coming through the forest. "There yew air!" she snapped angrily, shaking her impossibly blond hair. "Consortin' with disreputable people, yew varmint!"

"Aw, Daisy Belle," said Davy wearily. He passed his hand at her and she disappeared. "Funny thing," he said, looking redly sidewise at the voyagers. "Thet there phantasm jest won't stay a-vanished."

"Lonely old man," sneered Jocelyn. "Hah!" She flung the ship into high, slamming the door after the hermit of Razorback Crag.

III.

"Your clothes dried yet, honey?" called Ionic Intersection.

"Lay off the honey," warned Jocelyn, her eyes on the port. "You got yourself a man, even if you did lose him. How about it, Paul?"

"All dry," announced Gaynor, emerging in a suit that needed pressing. "Where are we?"

"By Clair's scale, about halfway from Earth to infinity. And the tracer's making noises like a dowager who's been eating radishes. Listen to the unmannerly creation."

Gaynor put his ear to the sounding-plate of the little plastic box. "Right," he stated grimly, "we're in the neighborhood."

"How about landing?" asked Jocelyn.

Gaynor flipped a coin. "We land. This twoheader never fails me; pulls us out of Nowhere into the Wherever."

His wife juggled briefly with the controls. Stars flashed again from the port. The counter's ticking swelled to a roar that filled the cabin. "Emphatic device!" yelled Gaynor through the din. He turned a screw on the case and shut off the counter action. "This is it, I expect."

"It?" Jocelyn dazedly inspected the planet they were nearing. "Give me a look at that thing."

"What's the matter with it? Or maybe you mean that city?"

"Exactly," she assured him, raising her hand to blot out the sight. "It's—awfully—big, wouldn't you say?"

"Few thousand feet high," commented Gaynor airily. "What's the odds?" He took over the controls and landed the ship.

"Ahg!" muttered Jocelyn to Io. "That extro-vert—landing us in the principal square with cars zipping past. Not that I'd mind if the cars were a little smaller than zeppelins. But does *he* care for my peace of mind? Not that worm. Did I tell you what he did one night last week? There I was ..."

"Look!" yelled Gaynor hastily, turning a little red. "See those ginks? Fifty feet high if they're an inch. What do you suppose they want?"

"I wouldn't even care to guess. Try the counter."

Gaynor turned on the little thing. For the brief-est moment it thundered, then went dead. "Blown out," muttered Gaynor. "Either that, or— " He tink-ered with it. "Nope," he announced finally, a bead of sweat coming out on his brow. "It's in commis-sion."

"Then why," asked Ionic Intersection plain-tively, "doesn't it sound?"

"I know, teacher," said Jocelyn. "It's fulfilled its whole function. It has counted faithfully and well as long as the object on which it was focused—that is to say, your husband's ship, more particularly, the protolens of that ship, obtained. It is now no longer functioning for the direct reason that the lens is no longer in existence. It was completely destroyed a few seconds ago—when the counter stopped sound-ing."

"But the ship won't run without the lens! And

the lens is mounted in solid quartz. How could they destroy the lens without destroying the ship?"

"They couldn't," stated Gaynor succinctly. "Keep calm, kid. If I know your husband, he's not in that ship. With his ship-rat instinct, he deserted it long ago. The pertinacious Pavlik won't fail you just yet. Meanwhile, dry your eyes—we have company. Give a look—out there." Gaynor stared through the port, glassy-eyed. "Giants," he continued strainedly. "Lots of them. Let's get out of here!" He kicked over the booster-pedal and very nearly started the drive-engines—but not before one of the giants had laid a two-ton finger on the ship and grasped it firmly between thumb and forefinger.

"No use busting gears against that thing." Gaynor cut off the motor and relaxed. "Any suggestions, babes?"

"Not one" said Jocelyn. "They seem to be talking— at least, the sky is clear; can't be thunder."

"Whu—what's that?" quavered Io, pointing. The port was completely filled by a colossal jelly-like mass that heaved convulsively. The blackish center seemed to be a hole of some kind through which they could look and see a dim cavern shot through with a strata of metallic matter, and honeycombed in its far rear with a curiously regular pattern of hexacombs. "Is it alive?"

"That," said Gaynor gently, "is an eye. And not at all an unusual one—just a big one. It's what yours would look like under a microscope. For God's sake, keep calm."

The eye withdrew and the *Prototype* clanged hideously with the din of a thousand bells as some colossal sledge crashed against their shell. "That," said Jocelyn as she picked herself from the floor, "could be the inevitable attempt to establish communication with the little creatures so unexpectedly arriving. She lifted a wrench. "They answer, thus." She rained blows on the shell of the ship until their ears rang.

"That's enough," said her husband removing

the wrench from her hands. "Now that you've succeeded in denting the hull all out of its streamlines. But maybe it did some good." They could hear the conversation thundering resumed; colossal feet stamped about the ship as it seemed to be surveyed from all angles.

"Awk!" shrilled Io as the *Prototype* lurched violently. Like peas in a bladder, they were shaken into the stern.

"Io," said Jocelyn sharply. "Would you mind—" she gestured the rest.

"Sorry," replied the brunette, arranging her clothes. "Anyway, your poor dear husband seems to be out." Jocelyn gave her a hard look. "I can take care of *him*," she retorted, climbing the steeply sloping floor, toward the water tank.

"Jocelyn," complained Gaynor reproachfully, "that wasn't fair—hitting me when I wasn't looking."

"I didn't," said his wife, busily changing the cold compress. "Your fifty-foot friends seem to be taking us for a ride in one of their Fallen Arch Sixes. You've just come to after an interval of about three hours. They keep looking in, and I think they're making dirty jokes." A titanic bellow of laughter rang through the ship. "See what I mean?"

"I don't see the joke," said Gaynor absently, holding his head. "What's Io doing?"

"Admiring the giants. She thinks the one in the middle has the cutest beard." Just then the vague drone of a colossal motor somewhere near them stopped.

"Journey's end, I take it? Or perhaps just a traffic light?"

"First stop thus far," said Jocelyn. The ship lurched again. "Up we go!" she cried gaily. "Better than a roller-coaster."

There was a brief, bumpy transition with admonishing grunts from the giants. "Easy there," warned Jocelyn. "Don't drop it more than two hundred feet—these animals might be delicate. Blunderbore, you dope—keep your end up—what're you doing, hanging on? There we are!" The ship settled and the seasick Gaynor groaned with relief. "Now what?" he asked tremulously.

"Now we get picked out and put on fish hooks, I guess. Think you'll wiggle?"

"Horrid woman!" he snapped, holding his head. And then something suspiciously like a can-opener poked through the shell of the *Prototype* with a screech of tearing metal. Jerkily it worked its way along the top of the ship, then twisted sidewise and opened a great gap in the frames. "Now we strangle?" worried Jocelyn. The air rushed out for just a moment, then the pressure seemed to equalize.

"Pfui!" sniffed Ionic Intersection. "Sulfur some-where. But breathable, this air. How do you feel, honey?" She caught a glance from Jocelyn. "Paul, I mean," she amended.

"Okay, I guess—hey!" squawked Gaynor as a pair of forceps reached down into the ship and picked him up by his coat collar, through the colossal rent in the *Prototype's* hide.

"Write me a post card when you get there, dear-est," called Jocelyn. "Oh well," she asided to Io, "easy come; easy go. But still I'd have—hey!" she squawked as the forceps made a return trip.

IV.

"No privacy," complained Gaynor bitterly. "No pri-vacy at all—that's the part I don't like about it. And that damned blue ray they use—insult on injury; Pelion on Ossa! The great lubberly swine implied that they needed a short-wavelength to see us at all. Oh the curs, the skulldruggerers!"

"Shut up," advised Jocelyn. "We seem to be here for some little time under inspection. What comes next I can't possibly imagine. The thing I don't like is that while you can talk yourself out of any given scrape, this presents peculiar difficulties, such as that they can't hear you for small green caterpillars, and even if they could, they couldn't because your voice is too high-pitched. You!" She turned accusingly on Ionic Intersection.

"Your husband has to go running out on us and get himself involved with these stinkers— "

"Now, Jos," said Gaynor placatingly, "the poor child— "

"Child, huh? I've a notion that you weren't as unconscious as you pretended when she landed in your lap. And if she's a child, I'm the gibbering foetus of a monkey's uncle!"

"Look!" said Gaynor hastily. "There comes another one." A colossal eye stared blankly at them, its jelly-like corona quivering horribly, the iris contracting like a paramecium's vacuole under a microscope.

"Nyaa!" taunted Jocelyn, thumbing her nose at the monstrous thing. "Bet you wish you were my size for an hour or two—I'd teach you manners, you colossal slob! Come on in here and fight like a man!" There was an elephantine grunt from the creature's mouth somewhere.

"No," said Jocelyn scornfully. "Not like him—" jerking a thumb at her husband—"I said a *man*."

"Now, Jos, really," began Gaynor.

Ionic Intersection looked up from her corner. "I'm hungry," she wailed.

"Hungry, hah?" asked Mrs. Gaynor. "Room Service!" she bawled. The eye reappeared. "Ah, they're learning. Now for the customary pantomime of starvation." She patted her stomach, pointed to her mouth, slumped to the floor, gestured as if milking a cow and chewed vigorously on nothing. "Think Joe up there will get it?"

"I hope so," worried Gaynor. "I could go for an outside amoeba myself. Which reminds me—do you think these ginks' cellular structure is scaled up like their bodies, or do you suppose their cells are normal size like ours—but much more plentiful?"

"Bah!" spat his wife. "Scientist! Why didn't I marry an international spy? I knew the nicest little anarchist once—full of consonants. I called him Grischa and he called me Alice. Always meant to ask him why, but they shot him before I had the chance. I wish they'd shot you instead. And your half-baked partner! And his blubbering wife!"

A tiny—about twenty feet—section of the netting avove their heads lifted off and an assortment of stuff fell at their fee. "Reaction?" suggested Gaynor.

"Food!" said his wife hungrily. She looked closer. "But what food! Note this object d'excrete—I'll swear its the leg of a ten-foot cockroach." As she spoke, the thing flopped convulsively. "Pavlik," she said coaxingly, averting her eyes, "put the thing away somewhere where I won't be able to see it, huh?"

Gaynor lugged the sticky horror to the netting that enfenced them and poked it through one of the holes. "All gone," he announced. "And the rest of the stuff looks almost appetizing. That is, if you've eaten as many things as I have in my academic career. Snails at the Sorbonne, blutwurst at Heidelberg, Evzones—I think it was Evzones—at the University of Athens— "

"Well, let's try it. What first? The—er—pickled—er things or the fried—they look fried—stuff?"

"Let's try it out first," suggested Gaynor, covertly indicating Ionic Intersection, whose eyes were buried in her handkerchief.

"Of course," murmured Jocelyn, sweetly. With a shudder she picked up something green and lumpy and brought it to the brunette. "Now, dear," she urged, "do try some of this delicious ragout de pferdfleisch avec oeufs des formis."

"Is it nice?" asked Io trustingly.

"Of course," said Jocelyn, watching like an eagle as Io bit into the thing. "How do you feel? I mean, how do you like it, sweet?"

"Delicious," said Io, tightening her clutch on the thing.

"That's all I wanted to know," snapped Jocelyn. "Give it back!" She wrenched it from the brunette, who broke out into a new freshet of tears, and sunk her teeth into the most promising of the green lumps.

"Tsk, tsk, such manners," chided Gaynor, "when there's ample for all. Here, Io," he said gently, bringing the little brunette an assortment of the green stuff.

"Quite full, you goat?" asked Jocelyn of her husband.

"Nearly." He reached for a brownish object; his arm fell halfway. "Can't make it," he observed. "Must be full. What happens now, wife of my heart?"

"Can't imagine," she assured him, studying her lips in the mirror of a compact.

"To hazard a guess," he said, looking up, "that forceps is intimately connected with our immediate futures. Here we go," he called down gaily as it lifted him high into the air.

A moment later, Jocelyn and Io joined him, via forceps. "Where are we?" wailed the brunette, looking around wildly.

"Keep off those coils," warned Gaynor. "Better just stand still. It looks like a twenty foot bowl lined with all kinds of electric junk in it."

He turned on the woman suddenly. "What's *that* you called me?" he mouthed furiously, working his hands.

"I didn't say anything," protested his wife.

"I didn't either," chimed in Io. "Has he gone crazy?" she asked Jocelyn.

"Hah!" she laughed loudly and vulgarly. "I won't even take that lead." She turned and surveyed her brooding husband. "What!" she squawked suddenly, turning on Io. "If you want my opinion that goes for you, too—double!" The brunette looked bewildered.

"Hold it, girls," said Gaynor. "Io didn't say a thing—I was watching her by—er—coincidence."

"Yeah," said Jocelyn. "You look out for those coincidences. Reno's still doing a roaring trade, I hear. But if Io didn't say it, who did?"

Gaynor pointed upward solemnly.

"Oh Paul, don't be a bore!" his wife exploded. "I didn't know I was married to a religious fanatic!"

"No," said Gaynor hastily, "don't get me wrong. I mean Joe or his friends. This thing, now that I consider it, looks like the well known thought transference-helmet we meet so often. Not being able to make one small enough for us, they put us into one of theirs. Now try opening your minds so maybe something more than subconscious insults from our captors may get through. Ready? Concentrate!"

They wrinkled their brows for a moment; Io giggled and cast a sidewise glance at Gaynor, who uneasily eyed Jocelyn, who gave Io a murderous look. "Heaven help you if I intercept another one like that, husband mine," Mrs. Gaynor warned.

"Must have been wholly subconscious," he replied. "Even I don't know what it was."

"I'd rather not tell you," said Jocelyn, "but your subconscious has a mighty lively imagination."

"Hush," said Gaynor abruptly. "Here it comes!" He squatted on the base of the helmet and shut his eyes tightly, his jaws clenched in an attempt to get over and receive.

"Paul!" said Jocelyn, alarmed.

"Quiet!" he snapped; "this isn't easy."

Thus, to outward appearances, practically in a trance, he remained.

"It must be wonderful to think like that," breathed Io.

"Yeah," agreed Jocelyn. "But all he's doing is getting us out of a jam, your husband's a real thinker—by just hopping off with suicide in his mind, he can get us into the jam. You ought," she continued witheringly, "to be mighty proud of your Art Clair. I just hope he turns up scattered from here to Procyon!"

The brunette did not, as Jocelyn expected, burst into tears again. There was a sort of quiet contempt in her voice when she spoke. "If you had any honesty or decency in your makeup you would remember that Arthur took this trip to force your husband out of his blind stupidity. Arthur's invention was a perfect success—it's you and your husband's fault we're stuck now, not his."

Jocelyn stared at her for a moment. "Blah!" she said. Then, with concern in her eyes, she watched the motionless form of Gaynor.

"God, that was awful!" groaned Gaynor. He relaxed and stretched his limbs. "I wish Art had been here—he was the psychologist of the team, ideally suited for a heavy load like I've been taking on for the last hour or so."

"What happened, Paul?" asked Jocelyn. "You didn't move—I was worried."

"Well," said Gaynor slowly, "it wasn't as awful as it probably looked to Outsiders. The hardest part was getting their thought patterns down clear. You know how hard it is to understand someone from a radically different speech area, even though he speaks what is technically the same language?"

"Yes," his wife nodded.

"Did it seem to come clear in your head suddenly?" asked Ionic Intersection.

"Right—that's how it was with our friends."

"Oh," said Jocelyn sarcastically, "so they're our friends, now, huh?"

"Yep. I talked them out of some silly notion they had of popping us into iodoform bottles. They're really not bad guys at all. As they explained it, they're rather hard pressed. It's the usual set-up, that you come on in history after history."

"Crisis?" asked Jocelyn, her eyes brightening. "Wow!"

"Exactly. Democracy against—the other thing. And exceptionally fierce in this case because our friends, the democrats, are far less in number than their enemies. Culturally and technologically they're well balanced. Just a matter of population that keeps them from winning. Our friends thought we were spies from the other side—who happen to be giants, too. They took the poor little *Prototype* for a deadly bomb—how do you like that?"

"I like it fine," said Jocelyn.

"Did you find out anything about Arthur?" asked Io quietly.

Gaynor hesitated. "I don't want to raise any false hopes," he said slowly, "but they have rumors—only the vaguest kind of rumors—of someone showing up in the enemy ship. From all accounts of the enemy camp, that someone's chances of long survival are none to good. That's all they could tell me."

"Too bad," mused Jocelyn. "Too, too bad. Paul, can you get in touch with them again—can you stand it?"

"No mistaken consideration, Jos," he replied. "What do you want me to ask the blighters?"

"I'd like to find out if there's any chance of our getting to see what might be the mutilated corpse of the late and lamented Mr. Clair."

"Let's join forces with them" spoke up Io. "Being small as we are, we can easily look for Arthur and assist them at the same time."

"I say yes—loudly and emphatically," agreed Gaynor. "Now if I can get a little silence around here, I'll go into my trance." He squatted on the floor and shut his eyes, droning: "Calling Joe ... calling Joe ... Gaynor calling Joe ... Come in, Joe ... what kept you?"

V.

Back in the relatively comfortable living quarters of the *Prototype*, which had been repaired during their absence, the voyagers were trying on their new thought-helmets. "As I understand it," said Gaynor, "one big difference between the good guys and the versa is this helmet business. I doubt very much whether the good guys realize just how much difference that makes. Thus:

"The common, everyday helmets, used by both good guys and bad are two-way, like a telephone circuit. Incoming and outgoing, both. Whereas these things we have, and which Joe and his friend have—albeit on a somewhat larger scale—are monodirectional. While wearing these helmets we can receive, but we can't send unless we want to very much. Get it?"

"Then," said Io thoughtfully, "they must have a two-way thought shield, not letting anything either in or out."

"Precisely. Both sides have that of course. And precious little good it is to anybody, either. How's yours, Jos?"

Jocelyn fitted the snug, gleaming little cap on her head with an uneasy smile. "Wow!" she exclaimed, reddening. "It seems to drag things up out of the subconscious—my own subconscious."

"Ah," said Gaynor. "Yes, that's because the things are so small. The theory that Joe's boys have is that the conscious thoughts are sort of long-wave—though millimicrons smaller than anything measurable—and that subconscious thoughts are super short-wavelength. I asked them about the center band, but they didn't have any opinions. Psychoanalysts and installation-engineers dance cheek to cheek, as it were, in this world. You can keep your ucs in line by voluntary means. That'll come to you after a while. Now how is it?"

"Okay. What now?"

"I'll send a test signal—without speaking, of course. You're supposed to catch it and tell me what it is. Ready?" Gaynor, at his wife's nod, frowned and shut his eyes. "That was it," he said at length. "What did you get, if anything?"

"Nothing at all."

"Did you catch anything, Io?" he asked worriedly.

The brunette nodded, and recited

There was a young fellow named Hannes
Who had the most horrible manners;
He would laugh and he'd laugh
Making gaffe after gaffe,
Spreading tuna-fish on his bananas.

"Exactly," said Gaynor. "But we'll have to try again. I'll send another one, Jos. See if you can get it this time."

She closed her eyes in concentration, then an instant later, recited

Willis, with a fiendish leer,
Poured hot lead in pappa's ear;
Sister raised a terrible fuss:
"Now you've made him miss his bus!"

"Right," said Gaynor with a sigh of relief. "Io, you seem to be doing all right, but let's see, Jos, if you can send one to me."

His wife leered and shut her eyes. A pause followed. "Well," she said relaxing, "what was it?"

Without comment, he recited:

In the cabin of Gottesman's Proto
Sherlock Holmes met the suave Mr. Moto;
You could tell by their air
They were looking for Clair,
Who had vanished, not leaving a photo.

"You got it," she approved.

"Yeah, but who's this guy Gottesman? Never heard of him."

"Just a guy I know," she replied with an absent smile. "You wouldn't be interested, Paul."

"No doubt. But you'd better not emit any more

loose talk about Reno when I happen to glance in Io's direction, my sweet.

"Be that as it may—we have a job to do, sort of. As I told you, the bad guys are under the thumb of some sort of War Council which was established as a special emergency three centuries ago, and hasn't been disbanded since. Because, the theory goes, the emergency still exists. Our job is to spy on these people—hence the helmets. Now, if you'll honor me—?" He crooked a courtly elbow at her; she accepted with a gracious smile, and they stepped from the ship, followed by Ionic Intersection, who had a secretive sort of smile on her face.

"Okay, Joe," Gaynor announced to the colossus towering above them. "We're off!" A tremendous hand gently closed about them, lifting the three of them high into the air. "Paul," said Io tremulously looking down, "you never said a truer word."

The trip had been a dizzy panorama of a colossal countryside glimpsed from the windows of a car of some kind, and views from the pocket of Joe as he wormed through the ever-so-carefully prepared breech-hole in the walls of the bad guys' city. And he had kept up a running commentary of information for their benefit:

"This car operates by a new kind of internal combustion. We reburn water. Something that can't be done on your world, I believe. . . . That ruin was once a sky-scraping building. This whole area was once one of our cities. We had to retreat in one grand movement on all fronts—they'd developed something new in electrostatic weapons, and manufacture of shields would have taken too long, longer than we had of time, at any rate. . . .

"The crisis, I suppose, is nothing new to travelers such as you. Once—before the war—we had the energy and initiative to spare so that we sent out a few ships such as yours—not protomagnetic, much cruder. Percentage of failure was rather high. And reports of the returned voyagers were not very en-

couraging. You see, control was mostly psychologi-
cal, so the ships were drawn to planets and dimensions whose make-up was most like our own. Highly
antithetic, invariably. We should have taken warning—it was too late. Everything seemed to slap down
on us all at once. The culminative nastiness of all
time seemed to pour out on our heads. Our nation—
country—whatever you call it—isn't a natural one.
No common language, no common cultural stream,
as the dear archaeologists like to say. We're exiles,
most of us. And though we can't get together long
enough to agree on most things, we're united on the
grounds of mutual defense—very nice in one way,
but if we happen to win, by some weird fluke, there's
going to be one hell of a squabble afterwards about
the technique of our government."

"What's the matter with the one you're using
now?" suggested Gaynor. "And what is it, by the
way?"

"That? Just the certain knowledge that if one
man does a wrong thing, the rest will go under. That
leads to an instinctive rectitude of decision where
necessary, and to the toleration of deliberation where
that is indicated."

"Virtually an early Wells utopia," murmured
Gaynor. The car stopped and they felt themselves
being transferred to another pocket of the monster.

"Now," continued the monster, "we're walking
right through a wall into the fortalice of our enemies.
I'm warning you now to be ready to be deposited on
little or no notice. I hope you'll be able to escape in
the confusion and get under cover before they pay
very cursory attention to the surroundings."

"What confusion?" asked Io.

"Why, this—approaching in the form of several
guards, friends. We're very near the council room.
We're in it, now— " The abrupt end of the thoughts
of their carrier brought sudden shock to the three
cowering in the dark of his pocket. They could hear
confused roarings and explosions, then a hand

yanked them out, none too gently, and they fell far to the floor.

"Come on," snapped Gaynor, "damn our size—can't see a thing!" He yanked Jocelyn and shoved Io under the ledge of a colossal piece of furniture; they crouched in a passage no more than three feet high to their senses.

"My guess," said Io, "is that Joe is a suicide, practically. He must have known he wouldn't get out of this alive. These people deserve to win, Paul."

Gaynor was still fretting. "Now," he growled, "I know what a fly feels like—can't see more than a couple feet before its proboscis and even then doesn't comprehend what's going on. Jos, it makes me feel stupid and unimportant. Let's all tune in on the War Council. Relax, and open your minds."

"Paul, I can't understand the setup," said Jocelyn worriedly. "Everything's confused. Who's that mind receiving and broadcasting without a thought of his own? I don't get it."

"That mind," said Io thoughtfully, "seems to be an idiot of some kind."

"Of course!" cried Gaynor. "The War Council hasn't got one-way helmets; this is their dodge. The idiot is under some sort of hypnotic control, I'd say offhand."

"Being lice, and double—or, if necessary, triple-crossers, they don't trust each other with the two-way helmets. They don't do things the easiest way—by language—hmm, that's rather odd, too."

"Maybe they don't all speak the same language," suggested Io.

"That would explain it. Then this system, even though roundabout, is quick enough. They telepath to the idiot, who telepaths it to the others, and so it goes. Simple in a complicated sort of way. Now maybe you'll be able to follow them."

He relapsed into brooding silence and tuned in. The thin, dry mind-voice of a councillor was discussing something utterly unintelligible in the way of high-order chemistry. All Gaynor got was, in a gloating tone at the very end: "—phenol coefficient of two hundred and ninety-eight, gentlemen!"

A murmur of mental congratulations, then, from another. "How do you produce the poison?"

"Hot poison, corrosive."

"Corrosive, then. How do you make it?"

More alien technical terms, then the second voice. "Thought so. Lovely idea, but not practical yet. Work on it, man—work on it! This is a war of money as well as spraying liquids. If we could wipe them out in one advance with your stuff, it would be okay. Otherwise, it isn't worth the money we'd have to put out for it. But work on it, nonetheless. Phenol coefficient two-nine-eight, you say? Very good...."

Then a sharp mind-voice of command. "Tactically, what is there to report? You—nothing? You—nothing? You?"

"Something, chief. No much, but something. How'd you like to hear that the new air-field's caved in the center?"

"Speak up, rot you! Has it or hasn't it?"

"It has. Somebody's error in Engineering No. Eight, Chief. That ought to affect plans considerably, eh, sir?"

"I'll decide that, young one. And somebody swings for that error; make a note of it. See who initialed the final plans for the beaming and poured metal."

"Right, Chief. Now—what's the big news, sir? What's the time for it to pop?"

There was something like a pleased smile from the mind-pattern of the commander, they thought. Gaynor concentrated furiously to catch the precious next words. "The advance? In three days. Three days exactly. I shouldn't call it crucial at all—simply the operation on which we've been planning for a full long time. Naturally it will be successful. We shall go now. See that the idea is taken care of, someone. You."

"I'll be back for him in a moment."

There was a tremendous shuffling of feet, and when Gaynor cautiously poked his head out of the shelter, the room was empty except for the idiot, who, face high up, was blank as a dumbbell.

"C'mon out, all," he called, giving Jocelyn a hand. "We can case the joint."

They essayed a little stroll along the baseboard, feeling futile as a jackrabbit. The shuffling of two enormous feet gave a pause; he looked up with some trepidation. "Awk!" he groaned. The idiot, a bright beaming smile of interest on his face, dove two hands like twin Stukas at them. The hands closed about the struggling humans, and they were swooped up and violently deposited in a dark, dismal spot.

"So this," said Jocelyn finally, "is what an idiot's vestpocket is like."

VI.

"Total blank," said Gaynor despairingly. "He doesn't radiate thoughts at all. Just a something like the noise of an electric razor, implying hunger and fatigue."

"Doesn't he have any opinions of us?" asked Jocelyn timidly.

"Not a one. Just picked us up out of some kind of reflex. No intention behind it at all; if he knew what he was doing, he's already forgotten about it. Oops!" Gaynor started. "They just took off his helmet, I suppose. Anyway the buzzing came to an abrupt end. Here we go!"

They jounced around wildly in the pocket of the idiot as he moved slowly and with great dignity out of the room. The three miniatures were too busy clutching onto the course fabric of the pocket's lining to wonder where they were going, in general. The motion stopped; they heard the gigantic thud of a door closing on an unprecedentedly big scale.

"Locked in, I surmise," mused Gaynor. The

pocket dropped like an elevator. "Hmm, he sat down."

"Shall we make a break now?" asked Io.

"Now or never; come on, it's over the top." Taking firm hold of the stuff of the pocket, he climbed carefully, hand over hand, popping his head finally over the pocket's top. Jocelyn and Io appeared beside him.

"Can't get the scale of things here," he complained bitterly. "Can't tell where we are—whether that's a chair or the floor. Anyway— " He let go and fell heavily to the plane below. The great bulk of the idiot's body was beside him like a cliff. From the noises, one hazarded that it was eating—not very daintily. His wife and Ionic Intersection hit the ground beside him.

"Easy does it," he cautioned, clasping a chair leg with every limb he had. Braking carefully, he slid far down to the floor, then picked Jocelyn and Io off the huge trunk as they followed.

"Thanks," said Jocelyn, brushing herself. "What now?"

"Under the door, I suspect,'" said Gaynor. "We make one very quick run for it. If the dope sees us moving, we're probably through for good."

"For good?"

"Yep," he nodded. "The thing's likely as not to step on us." Abruptly he kissed the two of them. "Now!" he whispered, and they scampered across the floor in a mad spring for the door, hundreds of feet away. The crack beneath it would be ample for escape.

Behind them was a stir and the crash of breaking pottery, like the crack in Krakatoa. "Oh Golly!" moaned Gaynor, catching his wife's arm and hurrying her on.

"Leggo!" she panted. "Keep running—I'll— " What she would have done remained unsaid. Blocking their way were the immense feet of the idiot. They stopped short and stood like statues. "Here it comes," murmured Jocelyn.

The idiot was going through some mighty complicated maneuvers, the sum total of which was to bring his face to the ground, about eight feet away from the miniatures. He was grinning happily.

"Paul," gasped Io, almost hysterically. "Look at his face!"

Gaynor and Jocelyn stared fascinatedly. "No," whispered Jocelyn, "no! It can't be. It just couldn't possibly be!"

"But it is!" said Gaynor. "That thing, idiot or no idiot, fifty feet high or not, *is my partner, Arthur Clair!*"

Gaynor clasped the little brunette's shoulders. "It's all right, Io, believe me, it's all right!"

"But—Pavlik—my Arthur couldn't be— "

"I always knew he was an idiot," marvelled Jocelyn, "but never in this sense—that is, precisely in this sense. Will he find us, Paul?"

Gaynor shook his head. "I think he'll forget us in short order and get back to his dinner. Then I act and act fast."

"How, Paul?"

"Clair's under hypnotic control. I don't know how he got to that size, Io, but he's very obviously been ordered to forget everything and act as a sounding board for the ginks in the War Council. Now if I can yell loud enough for him to hear me— "

"But what good will that do?" interrupted Mrs. Clair.

"Just this, Io: When Arthur and I were younger, and much foolisher, we were simultaneously addicted to hypnotism and practical joking. My idea of a practical joke at the time was to give Art some pretty silly orders and postsuggestions when he was under.

"He, being fundamentally a bright sort of cuss, had himself immunized to that kind of thing by having a professional give him a very solid conditioning—to come out of any hypnotic states at the mention of—among other things—my name."

"So if he can only hear your name he'll be all right?" asked Io excitedly.

"Yup. And here I go. I see our partner has reverted to type." Clair was licking porridge from the floor, where his bowl had broken.

In one quick scampering run, Gaynor darted out from under the ledge and made it to the idiot's head, with Io close behind him. He bawled out the words: "PAUL GAY-NOR!"

The idiot looked at him. "Why, Pavlik," it said with gentle concern. "How on Earth did you get here?"

"Arthur!" sobbed Io running toward him.

With a puzzled look on his face, Clair picked up his wife gently and brought her toward his face. Tenderly he caressed her hair with his fingertips. "What did you three do to yourselves?"

"Look, dope!" yelled Gaynor. "What do you remember last?"

"Oh, I remember everything. Including picking you up. And I have in my mind a complete record of the transactions of the War Council for the week I was used to replace their last idiot, who got a fuse blown somewhere. They had me under a limited kind of control—not really efficient. No oblivifaction coefficient at all. What do we do now?"

"Suppose," shrieked Jocelyn, coming out, "you get us to hell out of here. They won't stop you, will they?"

"Up to a certain point, no. They won't harm me at any rate. I have religious connotations of some kind, I think."

"Arthur—Paul—wait!" said Io. "I have an idea. You and Jocelyn go back to our friends; Art and I will stay here. Paul, you don't suppose these people have any screens against thought helmets, do you?"

"They haven't," said Clair. "What's on your mind, pet?"

"This. They'll be needing Arthur again soon when they start the offensive. And as far as they knew, he'll be as he was before.

"Only, I'll be in Arthur's pocket, relaying everything that comes into his mind to you back in the
citadel. While you relay to me the suggestions of
their War Council, or whatever they have like it.

"Do you get it, Paul? These birds will be getting
orders from their idiot, only it will be our orders!
That is—if you can make a screen, dearest."

Clair grinned. "I can."

"That's all very nice," protested Jocelyn, "but
how do Paul and I get out of here?"

"The idiot will get you over the wall— or under
it— " said Clair. "Before you go, you can send a
message to your friends to be waiting. I'll rig up an
apparatus so your thoughts won't be interrupted by
the wrong people—wow, the things I've learned
here, Pavlik!" He picked up the two and put them
in his pocket again. "Let's go," he said. "No one pays
any attention to the idiot in his time off, and they're
too busy to notice what he's doing anyway—unless
he yells for help."

And again the three went on a bumpy sort of
ride in the pitch blackness of Clair's pocket.

VII.

"It doesn't take you birds any time at all to go to
town on a new device once you have the idea," marvelled Gaynor as he fiddled with the dials of the spy-
screen several of Joe's friends had constructed. The
giants had a screen for their use—the room wasn't
long enough for Gaynor to be able to see it all— and
a small one had been made for the visitors.

"But it wasn't much of a problem," came the
thoughts of the giant Jocelyn had dubbed "Luke."
"As soon as you told us about it, it was quite simple.
We had all the makings—only thing is, it never occurred to us—or to them, either, apparently."

"What's the program?" asked Jocelyn.

"At the moment, we're getting the layout of their citadel, and the disposition of their forces. Luke and Oley here (Oley's the blond, sweet) are very busily engaged in making a map of the works—giving all the data we need."

"Their layout seems to be that of a seven-pointed star," mused Jocelyn. "No encircling rings of fortifications—just points."

"Probably all they need," said Gaynor. "Don't be too sure that there isn't a solid ring of some kind aroung their citadel. Wouldn't be at all surprised if those seven points weren't the terminals for a virtually unpenetrable vibrational barrier."

"But we had no trouble in getting through!"

"Only because they see no point in keeping it up constantly. They probably have some sort of detectors. Don't forget, Joe was discovered and disposed of in virtually no time at all after he got in."

Gaynor plugged in a connection. "Ah, here we are." The screen lit up to show an office where several giants, apparently of high rank in the enemy's forces, were also poring over war maps. As a light on the desk flared, they straightened up and took down what were obviously thought-helmets from a nearby rack."

"We do likewise," said Gaynor suiting his words to action.

"Then?"

"Then the fun begins. It'll work like this: I will be the mental sounding board for our side, little more than an extrapolated dimwit like my partner, Art Clair. As messages from their staff come to him, he shoots them over to me via Io and Luke and his friends pick them up. Luke and his friends decide whether the order will go through as is, or whether it'll be changed, and if so, how. In the meantime, Art's screening his mind against intrusion; soon's our misdirection gets to Art, he relays it to whoever it's supposed to go to."

"Sounds frightfully complicated," mused Jocelyn. "And won't those dopes get suspicious—won't it take time?"

Gaynor shook his head. "There's nothing as fast as thought." He made a final adjustment on the helmet. "If they're noticing such things, they may be aware of a slight pause, but it's doubtful that they'll notice—particularly when the fun starts. Which will be soon, now."

"This is all very ducky, husband mine, but what am I supposed to be doing all the time? Am I an orphan?"

"Suggest you watch the screens and keep in contact with our friends—never can tell when you might be able to make a bright suggestion. Matter of fact, you'll have to keep contact if you want to know where to send the spy-beams in order to see what's going on. Oh, it'll be exciting enough for your blood-thirsty tastes, pet. Just think of poor me—I won't know what's happened until it's all over."

"What! Won't you be in on this?"

"Yeah, with my mind a perfect blank."

"Huh," she snorted, "that'll be simple for you!"

Out of the bad guys' citadel came the air fleet, rank after rank of slender, black arrows, floating gracefully upward. In a few moments' time, thought Jocelyn, they would be over and beyond the outlying star-points and into the noman's land area. But at that precise instant, hell broke loose.

The neat, orderly arrangement of the first rank was suddenly shattered as four shells exploded simultaneously in its midst. Jocelyn gasped, twirled the dials of the screen seeking the source of the deadly fire. In a moment she had found it; a battery in one of the outlying fortresses had turned its guns upon their own air forces.

Misdirection with a vengeance, she thought. It worked beautifully when used upon such a set-up as the enemy had. Their whole training was that of blind obedience to superiors—she guessed what the orders must have been: attack and destroy the air fleet which has become a traitor to the fatherland.

The second wave had come up now, and, sizing up the situation (no doubt through the help of the idiot) quickly spread out, so as to offer the poorest possible target and dove for their attackers. There were no flashes from the great guns—they operated on springs. But their fire was deadly none the less; for all the maneuvering of the slender ships, black arrow after black arrow burst into shattered fragments.

By the time the third wave came up, the first two had been utterly disorganized, a few individual ships, diving toward the batteries and being blown out of the atmosphere. So far, not one hit by the fleet had been made, although several concerted dives had been attempted.

The third wave, it seemed would not be taken off guard. But Jocelyn, looking on and trying to out-guess the command, had forgotten the lovely possibilities of misdirection. The third wave did not attack the batteries at all; it hovered high above the citadel then dropped like hawks upon the ascending fourth wave of ships. As if, at a signal, all seven batteries directed their fire toward the citadel itself, raining devastating fire upon the vital sections.

Jocelyn tuned in upon the thought-waves to hear a veritable fury of hysterical commands and countercommands vibrating back and forth. At a sudden hunch, she sought out the room where the central command hung out with the idiot. She was amazed to find a heavy cordon of guards around the room, constantly being reinforced. She looked into the room itself, and rocked with laughter at the sight of Clair, sitting on a stool, drooling, a blank look upon his face. There was a faint bulge in his vest pocket—that would be Ionic Intersection.

The room was apparently soundproof to the nth degree. The central command sat around, a confident smirk upon their faces, watching maps, making marks upon them and nodding approvingly. Jocelyn took a closeup on the map and was amazed to discover that, according to it, the enemy air fleet was now approaching its objectives having smashed through the spheres of Luke's people. For a moment she stared disbelieving, then laughed again as the answer came to her. Of course! These sublime dopes weren't being let in on what was actually happening.

She flashed back to the scene of battle. The entire armada of black ships was now engaged in terrific battle with itself. Each squadron, she observed, had its own particular symbol, which helped. Because each squadron was attacking any and every other squadron.

Meanwhile, mechanized infantry was moving rapidly inward, upon itself. Paying little heed to the struggle in the sky, the infantry from the north side advanced upon, met, and locked in titanic combat with the infantry from the south. Land cruisers riddled each other with deadly fire while the soldiery on foot brought into play the "new weapon," the corroding mist. From little containers they squirted it far ahead of them and waited for the "enemy" to come on. It was the southern infantry that waited; the northern soldiery came forward.

Jocelyn stared for a moment in fascinated horror as the infantry moved into the terrain filled with the deadly corrosive mist, sat with her fists tightly clenched as the mist settled about them and slowly ate them away. There was no escape. The ghastly stuff was all-devouring. One drop upon any part of the clothing was sufficient, unless that bit could be taken off and flung away before it penetrated to the skin. She sat transfixed with the horror of it, then suddenly, switched to another scene. There was death and destruction in the skies, too, but it was swift and comparatively clear and painless.

The final scene came when the door of the central command's office was rudely shoved open, and a squad of soldiers came in. Before the amazed mucky-mucks could protest, they raised pistols and riddled them.

"Stop it!" Jocelyn's thoughts screamed out. "Their power's broken; put an end to the battle!"

"We've done just that," came back Luke's thoughts in answer. But Jocelyn didn't hear him; for the first time since adolescence, she was out cold in a genuine faint.

VIII.

"Do you people have any mass-decreasing stuff?" asked Gaynor, via telepathic helmet.

"No," sadly admitted Luke. "I fear you will have to go back to your universe as you are. Though I don't see what's wrong with Clair's size. I think it's a very distinguished size."

"Yeah," said Jocelyn in disgust. "You would."

The war was definitely over. They'd just finished a conference with emissaries from the former bad guys and a general session whereby arrangements would be made to help the former enemy reconstruct in return for certain processes which could be put to peacetime use was in the offing. Clair and Ionic Intersection had made their exit after the revolution, signalized by the shooting of the central command.

"But what," demanded Io, "caused Arthur to bloat up to his terrific size? I don't understand it."

"Perhaps," mused Clair, "it was because I took a different route to this plane. It's a marvel that the same thing didn't happen to you."

"So help me, partner," said Gaynor, "this is going to be awkward. Awkward as a bandersnatch—going around the good old USA with a colleague the size of a big house. I don't know what to do about it. And how we can get you back into the *Prototype* is also beyond me."

"What happened to *Proto Jr?*" asked Jocelyn.

"That went big, too. And unfortunately, I'm afraid it was blown up during the battle because it was right in the former bad guy's city. The counter lost focus when it swelled up, I guess.

"But this is what is known as a spot! Clair big and us normal— "

"Hold on a minute," interrupted Ionic Intersection. "Maybe that's not just so."

"Meaning what?" asked her husband.

"Meaning, my dearest, that maybe you're normal and we're small. Ever think of that?"

"Holy smokes!" gargled Gaynor. "You could be right at that." He clipped on his helmet and concentrated heavily.

"Yep," he said at length, "you seem to be right. And what does that dope Oley say but that they have mass-increasing stuff. And why didn't I ask him in the first place?"

"When do we bloat, then?" asked Jocelyn.

"Shortly, Oley says he'll have to get a special power line for the machinery. He can assemble that out of some stuff he has—hold on—what's— "

He felt a weirdly powerful grinding in his every cell, fiber, tendon, thread, and atom. Gaynor was growing. So, he saw, were Io and Jocelyn. Finally he stretched. "There, that's better. Much better. Lemme look at you, Jos— " His colossal mate smiled sweetly. "You giant," she said amiably, "I hope Io didn't guess wrong."

"Now," said Gaynor, "all we have to do is give the treatment to the Prototype, then we can scoot."

"Oh, you want to go?"

"Of course," said Jocelyn, "you don't think we want to stay here, do you?"

Clair and Io exchanged glances. "Io and I are staying," declared Clair, "but there's nothing to keep you two from making it back. Io's hasn't had any real mental exercise between the time we got back to Earth last and when you three landed here. And I must confess that I want to learn a lot more about these people, too.

"So, why not go back and leave us here—we'll call it a honeymoon."

"Come, my pet," said Gaynor gently, taking Jocelyn's arm. "I think they mean they want to be alone."

"You'll come back some day, Art?" asked Gaynor anxiously as the last batch of supplies were stowed away in the *Prototype*.

Clair nodded. "Sure." He took a familiar device out of his pocket. "Here's a duplicate of the counter. I don't want you and Jos stuck for my debts—you ought to be able to take care of them and yours, and have enough left over for the next few years' ice cream cones on what you get from this. Here are the plans." He tended Gaynor a small, thick envelope.

"Your analyser," he went on, "is set on me and mine on you. I've made a few improvements, on this pair. You can signal me with it, or vice versa. Nothing very complex, but enough so that I'll know if you want to come after me and vice versa.

"So remember, if you're in a tight spot and need me, just send out an SOS on this. I'll do the same if I need you. And if you're just coming my way, but there's no emergency, just send out the work CLAIR in regular morse on the dingus. I'll call GAYNOR in a similar situation for you."

"Good enough," murmured his partner. "So it's cheerio."

"Right. Bye, Paul."

Handshakes and osculations, then the door closed and the *Prototype* lifted up into the air.

"With the charts that Luke gave them, they ought to manage," mused Clair. "It's too bad in a way—I rather liked Pavlik."

"So did I," agreed Io. "Perhaps his wife will grow up some day. Then I'll be glad to see Jocelyn again."

"Oh—oh," muttered Gaynor at the controls of the *Prototype*, "there's something familiar about this section of space."

"Yer dern' tootin' they is!" snapped a familiar

voice. "Jumpin' Jehosophat, but caint an' old man hav any peace a tall? Hey! What happened ter the pretty gal with the brown hair?"

"She found her husband," explained Gaynor. "Honest, Mr. Canter, we weren't aiming to intrude. We're on our way home now."

"Weeel, reckon as haow yer might as well be sociable sence yer here. C'mon over 'n' see the new city I built after ye left the last time."

Gaynor followed the hermit's instructions and shot the *Prototype* in the directions stated. "Paul!" gasped Jocelyn suddenly, pointing a shaking finger, "Look!"

"Ulp!"

Before them stretched a city, but what a city! Huge buildings in the shapes of cones with needle-tips, balanced upon each other, cubes, hexagons, spheres, and every impossible and possible geometric shape. A riot of angles and slopes.

"Take it away," gasped Jocelyn weakly.

"Up here," came the hermit's voice. They looked to see Davy perched on a large sphere rolling along a zigzaggy road atop a tremendously high wall. Beside him sat the yellow-haired girl in the gingham dress they'd seen before.

"Gawd," muttered Gaynor, "I think I need some of that corn likker—without a hose."

"You and me both," agreed his wife. "Mr. Canter," she called, "I thought you were all alone?"

"So'd I," came back the response. "But this consarn phantasm here jest won't stay a'vanished—an' I reckon as haow I don't perticulerly want it ter, anyhaow." He cackled lustily.

"Ye kin tell me all abaout yer trip after we look araound a bit. Haow d'yer like my city. Built it after a pitcher thet thet feller Billikin had with him. Non-ob-jec-tive he called it."

"But we object!" gasped Jocelyn. She dashed to the controls and applied full power to the *Prototype.*

"Consarn!" muttered the ex-hermit of Razorback Crag to his yellow-haired consort as the *Prototype* vanished, "some people jest don't have no manners nohow!"

AFTERWORD

In 1941 the Japanese creamed Pearl Harbor, and by the early part of 1942, it became clear to all of us that our interesting and developing world was being derailed onto a quite different track. Cyril found work as a war-industry machinist in Connecticut. He moved there with his new wife (a young femmefan called Mary G. Byers, by whom in time he had two children), and we lost touch for a while.

Around March of 1943 Cyril turned up in New York again. He had enlisted in the Army, in a special program for machinists which made him the envy of all draft-bait. It would give him sergeant's stripes as soon as he finished basic training, and keep him busy repairing artillery well behind the lines instead of firing it, and being fired at, closer up. I had also volunteered, and was waiting for my orders. So the two of us stepped out for a drink to celebrate, which led to another drink, which led to one of the two drunkest nights I have ever spent in my life. (The other, six or seven years later, was also with Cyril.) When we woke in the morning, we shook hands tremblingly, not with emotion but with triple-distilled essence of terminal hangover. And Cyril went off to war, and so, a couple weeks later, did I.

We exchanged a little V-mail from time to time, but we didn't see each other again, or of course collaborate on anything, until the war was well over; but that belongs in **Critical Mass**.

203

ABOUT THE AUTHORS

FREDERIK POHL is a double-threat science fictioneer, being the only person to have won this field's top award, the Hugo, as both a writer and an editor. As a writer, he's published more than 30 novels and short story collections; as an editor, he published the first series of anthologies of original stories in the field of science fiction, Star Science Fiction. He was, for a number of years, the editor of two leading magazines, Galaxy and If. His awards include four Hugos and the Edward E. Smith Award. His interests extend to politics, history (he's the Encyclopaedia Britannica's authority on the Roman Emperor Tiberius), and almost the entire range of human affairs. His latest novel is JEM.

CYRIL M. KORNBLUTH began writing science fiction for publication at the age of fifteen, and continued to do so until his early death in his mid-thirties. In his own right, he was the author of four science fiction novels, including The Syndic, a number of works outside the science fiction field and several score of the brightest and most innovative shorter science fiction pieces ever written. Some of his short stories and novelettes have been mainstays for the anthologists and have also been adapted for television production. His collaboration with Frederik Pohl has been described as "the finest science fiction collaborating team in history." Together, they wrote seven novels and more than thirty short stories. Among their works are such classics as Wolfbane, Gladiator-at-Law, The Space Merchants and Before the Universe.

OUT OF THIS WORLD!

That's the only way to describe Bantam's great series of science fiction classics. These space-age thrillers are filled with terror, fancy and adventure and written by America's most renowned writers of science fiction. Welcome to outer space and have a good trip!

FANTASY AND SCIENCE FICTION FAVORITES

Bantam brings you the recognized classics as well as the current favorites in fantasy and science fiction. Here you will find the beloved Conan books along with recent titles by the most respected authors in the genre.

☐	01166	URSHURAK	
		Bros. Hildebrandt & Nichols	$8.95
☐	13610	NOVA Samuel R. Delany	$2.25
☐	13534	TRITON Samuel R. Delany	$2.50
☐	13612	DHALGREN Samuel R. Delany	$2.95
☐	11662	SONG OF THE PEARL Ruth Nichols	$1.75
☐	12018	CONAN THE SWORDSMAN #1	
		DeCamp & Carter	$1.95
☐	12706	CONAN THE LIBERATOR #2	
		DeCamp & Carter	$1.95
☐	12970	THE SWORD OF SKELOS #3	
		Andrew Offutt	$1.95
☐	14321	THE ROAD OF KINGS #4	$2.25
		Karl E. Wagner	
☐	11276	THE GOLDEN SWORD Janet Morris	$1.95
☐	14127	DRAGONSINGER Anne McCaffrey	$2.50
☐	14204	DRAGONSONG Anne McCaffrey	$2.50
☐	12019	KULL Robert E. Howard	$1.95
☐	10779	MAN PLUS Frederik Pohl	$1.95
☐	13680	TIME STORM Gordon R. Dickson	$2.50

Buy them at your local bookstore or use this handy coupon for ordering:

START A COLLECTION

With Bantam's fiction anthologies, you can begin almost anywhere. Choose from science fiction, classic literature, modern short stories, mythology, and more—all by both new and established writers in America and around the world.

Bantam Book Catalog

Here's your up-to-the-minute listing of over 1,400 titles by your favorite authors.

This illustrated, large format catalog gives a description of each title. For your convenience, it is divided into categories in fiction and non-fiction—gothics, science fiction, westerns, mysteries, cookbooks, mysticism and occult, biographies, history, family living, health, psychology, art.

So don't delay—take advantage of this special opportunity to increase your reading pleasure.

Just send us your name and address and 50¢ (to help defray postage and handling costs).

BANTAM BOOKS, INC.
Dept. FC, 414 East Golf Road, Des Plaines, Ill. 60016

Mr./Mrs./Miss_____
(please print)

Address_____

City_____State_____Zip_____

Do you know someone who enjoys books? Just give us their names and addresses and we'll send them a catalog too!

_____

Mr./Mrs./Miss_____

Address_____

City_____State_____Zip_____

_____

Mr./Mrs./Miss_____

Address_____

City_____State_____Zip_____

FC—9/78